CHRISTMAS WITNESS PROTECTION

MAGGIE K. BLACK

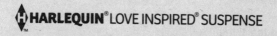

HARLEQUIN® LOVE INSPIRED® SUSPENSE

Recycling programs
for this product may
not exist in your area.

LOVE INSPIRED BOOKS

ISBN-13: 978-1-335-23239-7

Christmas Witness Protection

www.Harlequin.com

Printed in U.S.A.

The bricks are fallen down, but we will build
with hewn stones: the sycomores are cut down,
but we will change them into cedars.
—*Isaiah* 9:10

To Zachary. Thanks for the left hook.

ONE

It was a week until Christmas, and the early morning sky was every bit as cold and gray as the icy waters of Lake Ontario and the concrete loading docks that surrounded the car now transporting Corporal Holly Asher to her new life in witness protection. Her eyes flickered to the passenger-side mirror as another car came into view on the empty road behind them.

A tremor of warning brushed her spine.

"That looks like the same car I saw parked outside the safe house this morning," Holly said. "I think we're being followed."

Officer Elias Crane, the gray-haired witness protection officer in the driver's seat beside her, cut a glance to the rearview mirror. He frowned. "It's fine."

No, it really wasn't. Her gut told her something was wrong—very wrong—and after surviving two tours of duty overseas on a combination of faith and intuition, she wasn't about to start ignoring either now. Something about the Royal Canadian Mounted Police detective had had Holly on edge ever since Elias had woken her up at the safe house before dawn and given her exactly five minutes to get into the car. She'd done it in four, including an external sweep of the vehicle, which he'd told her wasn't necessary considering it was unlikely "anyone would go to too much trouble to stop someone from testifying in some government inquiry about a handful of misplaced weapons."

That was the moment she'd first felt her jaw set. It had been far more than just a handful of weapons and they hadn't been misplaced so much as illegally bartered, sold and given to warring factions by one of the most respected generals in the Canadian military. It was an international scandal, one that had the potential to ruin General Alberto "Bertie" Frey's career. Holly had grown up in a military family and dedicated her life to serving her country. After a decade of exemplary service, she'd agreed to come forward, testify in the upcoming inquiry against her former mentor and explain the best she could exactly how a man as beloved as General Bertie had somehow allowed dozens of Canadian military firearms to end up in the hands of warring desert families in a remote area of the world where the Canadian military was deployed. For that, she'd been treated like a pariah by some of the people she'd served alongside and had her reputation dragged through the mud online. Then had come the final breaking point—three thugs had jumped her one night in downtown Ottawa and tried to intimidate her, later claiming to police that some stranger had paid them to show her just how bad her life could get if she didn't keep her mouth shut. But they'd clearly underestimated the strength and power of the woman they were trying to scare out of testifying.

Even then she wouldn't have delayed deployment on

a third tour of duty or gone into witness protection if the RCMP hadn't insisted and the inquiry hadn't wanted to risk losing their star witness.

"I'm telling you it's the same car." She opened the sun visor mirror and took a better look, glancing past her own short-cropped black hair and the dark shadows that framed her green eyes. She couldn't see the driver's face in the darkness, but something about the sense of alert tension that seemed to radiate through his muscular arms and broad shoulders was anything but forgettable. "Could be a potential hostile."

"This is Canada, not Afghanistan." A chuckle slipped from Elias's lips, and Holly felt her spine stiffen. He gestured to the rearview mirror. "And that's just Detective Wilder. He's got a bit of a burr stuck in his fur about our drive."

"Why is he concerned?" she asked. "Has he been assigned to me, as well? Is there something wrong with my new temporary identity?"

The irritation that flashed in Elias's eyes told her the answer to the third question at least was no.

"Look, Corporal, it's fine," he said. "Can I call you Hildy?"

"No." Because it wasn't her name and she'd never been one for being called anything other than who or what she was. Her given first name was Hildegard, an old-fashioned family name shared by both her mother and grandmother. Her parents and very closest friends had always called her Holly, in part because she was born on Christmas Day. For everyone else in her life Asher would do. "Either Asher or Corporal is fine."

"Well, then, just learn to relax, Corporal, or it's gonna be a really long drive."

But how could she relax when something inside kept telling her something was wrong?

Help me, Lord. Something's not right. I can feel it. Help me know what it is and what to do about it.

A phone began to ring. She reached in vain for the cell that used to be in her pocket before she'd entered witness protection, and then realized it had to be Elias's. The officer yanked his phone from his own pocket and her eyes barely caught the name on the screen before he held it to his ear. *Det. Noah Wilder.*

"Back off, Wilder," Elias said. "I've got it covered. I don't need your help. I've been doing this since before you were in diapers and you're not even supposed to be on active duty!"

She didn't hear whatever answer Detective Wilder gave, but it seemed to be taking him a long time to say it. Elias was still driving with his phone to his ear and one hand on the steering wheel. Then he wedged the phone into his shoulder and his left hand darted out of sight. A loud and sudden click resounded through the car. Officer Elias had activated the child safety locks. He'd locked her in? Why had he locked her in? Elias swerved up an on-ramp and onto the elevated highway that ran through Toronto's downtown core. For a moment, the city spread out below her and skyscrapers pressed in around them. Then he darted down another ramp and back into a maze of docks and warehouses. Green and red cardboard letters in the windows of an ugly brick building wished her a Merry Christmas. She glanced back. The blue car had stayed on the highway and was now traveling parallel to them on the road above.

"You were wrong, plain and simple," Elias said. "The safe house was clean, the route wasn't contaminated and— Yes, I'm sure it's really her! I'm not about to pick up some imposter!"

He said the last word so loudly it seemed to reverberate inside the car. Warehouses hemmed them in on either side. Fleeting glimpses of ships docked in Toronto's harbor rose to her right, through the narrow, vertical slits between buildings. He turned down another, even narrower street, and though the man was old enough to be her grandfather, her own years of tactical experience made the hair stand up at the back of her neck. Not only did he not take her, or apparently Detective Wilder, seriously, he'd chosen a route with terrible lines of sight.

"You know, Corporal," Elias started, and it took her a second to realize he was now talking to her, "sometimes you've got to ask yourself if whatever stand you're trying to make is really worth all the trouble it's gonna put you through."

Gunshots split the air to their left, taking out the tires and shattering the driver's and back seat windows in a spray of bullets and broken glass. The phone fell from Elias's hand. His lifeless body slumped over the steering wheel. The vehicle swerved wildly.

No one was driving the car!

"Help me, God!" The words flew from her lips as she lunged for the wheel and fought to straighten the car. But the vehicle began to speed faster, as the pressure of Elias's full weight landed hard on the accelerator. She yanked her seat belt off, then threw her leg over the center console, kicking his foot off the pedal and pressing her own on the brake. The car spun on the icy ground. She clenched her jaw and tried to force the wheels to the right. But they reached a lamppost first, taking out the front of the hood as the vehicle slid into it. Her head slammed against the dashboard, then her body landed back against the seat. Pain filled her skull. The sound of a horn filled her ears as Elias fell against it.

"Hello? Hello?" A male's voice, deep and disjointed, floated up from somewhere below her. "Are you there?"

She pulled herself back into the passenger seat, checked Elias's neck for a pulse and couldn't find one. *Lord, have mercy on Elias and those who love him.* Then she felt around on the floor behind her for the phone.

"Hello?" She'd snatched it to her ear so quickly nausea swept over her. "Hello?"

"Corporal Hildegard Asher?" Detective Wilder's voice was warm and concerned, with just the faintest hint of a growl, and for some reason made her think of the protective wolf character from a book she'd loved as a kid.

"Speaking," she said. She slid the phone into the crook of her neck and carefully pulled Elias's service weapon from his holster.

"I'm Detective Noah Wilder," he said. "You can call me Noah. Are you okay? Where are you? Where's Detective Crane?"

"Detective Crane was shot and appears to be deceased."

She heard Noah whisper a prayer as she looked around. Her head was pounding, and it seemed to be affecting her ability to focus. Brick buildings and gray empty streets filled her gaze through the maze of broken glass. Noah's blue car was nowhere to be seen.

"Our vehicle was shot, and we crashed," she added. "I'm as okay as can be expected. But I can't see any street signs. Hang on, I'll go search the area."

"No, stay in the car," he said. "Wait there, until I can find you and assess the situation."

Her eyes rolled. She was just fine assessing the situation on her own, thank you very much, and then she could help him locate her and brief him better on his arrival. If only her head would stop pounding.

"Don't worry," Noah added. His voice softened. "It's all going to be okay. What happened?"

She opened her mouth to tell him, then closed it again. It had all happened just seconds before and yet somehow her mind was fuzzy.

"Gunshots came from our left," she said. "I didn't see the shooter."

"And then?" he asked.

"Then the vehicle lost control. I had to grab the wheel and force it to stop. We crashed."

And she'd hit her head. Motion dragged her attention back to the window. She looked up. A white cop car was pulling into the alley in front of her. A slim, uniformed officer sat behind the wheel. In recent years, Toronto police had slowly started swapping out their signature white cars for nondescript gray cruisers that blended perfectly into the dreary city streets in winter. But this one was an older model, its white hood reflecting the dim street light against the predawn sky. She glanced to the mirror. A second police vehicle was pulling up behind. It, too, contained just one officer—a large figure in a peaked uniform cap. "The cops are here. I'm going to go talk to them."

She grabbed the handle and pushed the door open.

"Wait! No! Stay in the car!" Noah's voice rose. "They might not be cops!"

What? What did he mean by that?

"What do they look like?"

"The cops?" she asked. "One's big. One's skinny. I can't really see their faces or give you much of a description from this distance."

Tires screeched. The vehicles ahead and behind her surged forward, as if both drivers were mashing their accelerators at once. They were coming up fast on either side, trapping her in the middle. She leaped from Crane's ruined car and started to run, feeling another wave of nausea sweep over her. *Help me, Lord!* The cruisers roared closer. She rolled, tucking her body tight and desperately hurling herself out of the way. The phone fell from her hand. She heard the screech of metal smashing hard against metal. Slush and dirt flew, spraying over her.

She lay still for a moment, shivering on the cold ground, urging her body to rise. Then she heard footsteps running toward her.

"I'll grab the phone and laptop, you grab the girl." The voice was thin, high-pitched, and made her think of a weasel. Then large, rough hands grabbed Holly. "We can use her."

RCMP Detective Noah Wilder scanned the cold, dark Toronto streets for any sign of Elias's car. The officer's phone was dead, Corporal Asher was gone and he'd lost sight of the vehicle when the overpass had turned slightly to the north. But he'd heard the sound of gunshots, and a car crash had split the morning air.

He never should've done what Crane wanted and backed off. Yes, the old officer had served for so long he'd twice declined retirement and now chose his own assignments. But he was also too set in his ways and didn't understand the nature of dark web threats. Not that Noah was exactly an expert, but he had an excellent source. One that had told him there'd been chatter in the seedier corners of the internet that a pair of cyber terrorists, called the Imposters, was going to hijack Corporal Asher's witness protection transfer.

But why? And what for? What would a pair of notorious dark web hackers and thieves want with a military corporal? He still had no idea. He just wished he was wrong.

Noah opened his window. Cold wind and the smell of burning fuel assailed him at once. For a moment the sound of the crash still seemed to bounce and echo off deserted buildings in the frosty morning air. Then they faded, and silence descended again. He pulled up one street and down another. Three cars came into view, mashed and tangled together. There were two white cop cars, with Crane's vehicle in the middle.

Noah stopped the engine, pulled his weapon from its holster, thankful he'd maintained his authorization to carry a handgun. Then he leaped out and ran toward the wreck. Thick snow swirled down from the sky above him. The passenger door and trunk of Elias's vehicle were open. The elderly officer lay against the steering wheel, and even at a glance Noah could tell he hadn't made it. Corporal Asher was nowhere to be seen. Sets of footprints spread across the ground were quickly disappearing in the blanketing snow.

God, please help me find her.

He grabbed his phone and hit a number. Seth Miles answered before it had even rung once. "Hey, Noah? I'm getting intel that the Imposters might be posing as cops."

Seth was what was known in the tech industry as a "white hat" computer hacker because he only used his considerable powers for good. He was notorious for taking down and exposing abuse and corruption in places of power, starting with his own violent military general father. For years Seth had tried to be more of a heroic outlaw, hacking at will, infiltrating various criminal organizations and tipping off law enforcement, while skirting laws that got in his way. Then some violent criminals, linked to organized crime, had kidnapped him, hoping to use him for their own purposes, and Noah had saved his life.

"Too late," Noah said. "Looks like they already found Officer Crane and Corporal Asher. Are you tapped into whatever area surveillance you can get of the Port Lands around the water filtration plants—"

"That would mean bending the terms of my witness protection agreement—" Seth started.

"Understood," Noah cut him off. He'd been responsible for Seth's protection for eighteen months and knew all too well the terms he'd agreed to, as well as his habit of skirting them. Noah didn't much like it, but that was a battle he'd have to save for another day. "But you already opened this can of worms when you tipped me off and I'm asking not instructing. Right now you're an informant in a possible murder and possible kidnapping. I'm looking at a car crash, a missing whistleblower and a dead RCMP officer. I think the Imposters took Hildegard."

"Sorry, on it." Seth took a sharp breath. Then came the sounds of typing. "I think her friends call her Holly, by the way. I'm guessing it's because she was born on Christmas."

Holly.

Noah's mind flashed to the image of the strong, slender and attractive woman with dark hair and piercing green eyes he'd seen in her file. Yes, that name suited her better.

"Rumor is she hates being called Hildegard," Seth added.

"You know her personally?" Noah asked.

"I know of her," he said. "We both grew up military, went to the same high school for a year and even as a teenager she had a reputation for being exceptionally talented at both precision shooting and hand-to-hand combat."

"What can you tell me about the Imposters?" Noah asked.

"They're cyber terrorists," Seth said. "In it for the money and not ideology. It's believed there are only two of them. The huge hulking one who manhandles and hurts people goes by the handle the Ghoul. The other is a lot smaller and goes by the Wraith. They say he's Canada's second best hacker."

No guess who Seth thought the best was.

"They go after very large-scale targets," Seth added.

"Hundreds of thousands if not millions of dollars. They're ruthless and mercenary. In it for money and destruction. They've been known to both wear disguises and kidnap people to use online as proxies, before killing them. It's said that no one has ever seen either of their faces and lived."

The typing stopped.

"Okay, I think I've got you," Seth said. "Skipped the street cameras and went for piggybacking on a satellite. Just zooming in. Now I can see you. What do you need?"

"Everyone. Local police, RCMP, ambulance and our missing whistle-blower," Noah said. "Any hostiles in the area?"

"Nope, you're all clear," Seth said. "I'm trying to track where the Imposters took Holly now."

Hopefully, they were still on foot and hadn't gotten far. In the meantime, Noah would go old-school.

"I've got footprints," he said, "and I'm going to follow them. If you see anyone or anything coming my way, let me know."

"Will do." Seth kept typing.

Noah started toward the footprints, weapon at the ready, following the faint and fading indentations in the snow. How had they managed to take her alive? When he'd been parked down the road from her safe house, he'd watched as she walked out to Elias's car and insisted on doing a visual sweep of it herself, like a pro. Then she'd glanced his way and for one fleeting moment, her eyes had locked on his face, and it was like someone had sucked all the air from his lungs. Corporal Holly Asher was beautiful in a way he'd never expected from her file, with cropped black hair that perfectly framed her face and a strong, straight, almost regal bearing. Her military file alone had been enough to catch his eye. She was brilliant, talented, decorated and brave. But there was something else to her, too, a quality that had made it hard to look away.

Just keep fighting, Holly. Wherever you are, just keep fighting until I can get to you.

"Give me something!" Noah reached the end of the alley and looked around. The snow fell heavier now, wiping out any hint of footprints there might have been. He heard more keyboard taps. Each second ticked by, longer than he could stand.

"Got her," Seth said. "Warehouse. One street over to your right and three doors down."

"On it." Noah started running. "I need you to call this in for me. Call everyone. Toronto cops. RCMP. The whole shebang."

"Already done." Seth sounded worried. "But those aren't secure lines. Anyone good enough to pull this off can hack into them."

"I know." Noah reached the next corner and dived into an alley. Dirty red and gray brick hemmed him in on either side. "But we have to do this by the book the best we can."

A row of doors appeared to his right.

"I just can't guarantee who you're going to get showing up," Seth said, "and whether they're going to be real or Imposters. Also, I think there could be a leak within the RCMP. Either that or someone in the military who happened to know everything about Holly's protection detail and Elias's movements. I just can't see any other way the Imposters would've gotten enough information to set this up and kidnap her this way. There has to be a mole. Or some other way the RCMP has been infiltrated."

"I figured," Noah said. "That's why I'm also going to need an extraction team."

Fellow undercover RCMP detectives, who he knew were in the city, people he trusted with his life, who'd been through their own tricky and dangerous assignments and survived. Officers who, like him, were currently off active duty or on leave, so couldn't have been tainted by whatever mole or leak there might be inside the RCMP. "Get me Mack Gray, Jessica Eddington and Liam Bearsmith."

"Assemble the renegade detectives," Seth said. "I like it. Should I worry that none are currently on active duty?"

"No," Noah said. It was none of his business, any more than the personal reasons he was technically on vacation were theirs. Liam was on six months medical leave after being beaten into a short-term coma when his cover was blown. He looked as strong as an ox on the outside, but Noah suspected that whatever had happened had left lingering scars. As for Mack and Jess, all he knew was that both were facing some kind of review for something that had happened on a past assignment. "Just be thankful we have three of the best cops in the entire world available to help us out of this mess."

"What do I tell them?" Seth asked.

"To get somewhere close and stand by."

"And what do I say if they ask about my connection to all this?" Seth asked. "You know I don't work for you."

Like Seth hadn't volunteered for this the moment he'd brought it to Noah's attention.

"Tell them you're that famous hacker guy I once rescued from the trunk of a car and dragged safely through a hail of bullets."

Seth chuckled. "Do they know *you're* not on active duty?"

Noah didn't answer. He'd landed an important promotion within witness protection, only to discover there was a glitch in gaining the necessary higher level security clearance due to a major financial mess his foster brother Caleb had gotten him into. It had left him in a bit of a limbo and, for now, he was using up vacation time and not being assigned any new cases until he decided what to do about it. But that didn't mean he wasn't cleared to work.

On the plus side, being off the clock had given him the freedom to take a personal interest in Elias's transfer of Holly, when Seth had tipped him off that there might be a problem. And while Elias clearly hadn't wanted Noah butting his nose in his assignment—let alone showing up in person when Elias hadn't taken him seriously—he was really thankful he had.

Noah reached the third door. His gloved hand grabbed the industrial handle and pulled. It didn't budge. "Am I at the right door?"

"Yup," Seth said.

"Got it." Noah reared back and kicked hard. The door flew open. A long dark hallway lay before him.

"Just to be clear," Seth said. "Once you go in there, I won't have eyes. I might not even have ears, depending on how deep the building goes and if it has a signal jammer. You'll be on your own."

"Got it," Noah repeated. He'd never minded working alone, and he didn't want the sound of him talking on the phone, or even listening to someone on the other end, potentially alerting anyone he might want to sneak up on. "Put me on hold, assemble the troops, stay ready and I'll get back to you soon."

"Sounds good. Stay safe."

"I'll try." Noah ended the call, put his phone on silent and slid it into his pocket. Then he raised his weapon high. *Help me, Lord. I don't know what I'm walking into.*

Noah stepped into the warehouse. Darkness enveloped him. He crept down the hallway, following the lines of the walls as they curved and twisted deeper into the building. His rubber-soled boots moved silently on the concrete floor.

The gray, rectangular outline of a slightly open door finally appeared ahead. Noah sucked in a breath and prayed, eased the door open and stepped through slowly. He emerged onto a catwalk overlooking a warehouse. Cardboard boxes and tarp-covered pallets filled the space below and were piled high around him.

And then he saw Holly.

The corporal sat in a chair facing him, alone in a gap in the middle of the warehouse. Her hands seemed bound behind her back, but her legs were free. She looked up at him, her face full of strength and determination. His heart lurched.

Then her eyes darted to her right and she gave a slight nod, as if acknowledging he was there and indicating she wanted him to see something. He stepped forward, following her gaze, and dread surged inside his core as he saw what she was gesturing to.

It was a video camera.

TWO

A large man stepped into view, blocking Noah's sight of Holly and the camera. He was huge, tall and broad, dressed in a dark navy police uniform with a hat pulled low. This would be the Ghoul, Noah guessed. He felt his breath tighten in his chest, willing the man to move. He had to see Holly's face for just a moment longer. He had to know she'd seen him and that she knew he was there. He needed her to know that he would help her, even if he didn't yet know how he was going to do that.

Holly was at least two stories below him and several rows of boxes and shipping containers away. Noah's phone buzzed in his pocket. He stepped back and reached for it, thankful he'd put his usual ringtone on silent and expecting to see Seth's name or that of a fellow officer. Instead the name Dr. Anne Reed filled the screen. He hesitated. While he was growing up, his family had fostered over a dozen children for different lengths of time.

He'd gotten to know Anne as a teenager, when she'd started dating his foster brother Caleb. Due to her own rough family life, she'd quickly become a nearly permanent fixture in the Wilder home. Anne and Caleb had had a baby together at eighteen and been married at nineteen. She was the closest thing Noah had ever had to a sister, and he considered their children his niece and nephew. But while Anne had excelled in school and become a medical doctor in her midtwenties, Caleb had careened through life, squandering away every cent and advantage he'd been given, relapsing after two stints in rehab for a gambling addiction and bouncing from one personal mistake to the next. His relationship with Anne was strained. He'd left her and the kids more than once, before always deciding to come back and give it another try. Caleb had also cut off all contact with Noah almost a year ago thanks to a joint business venture that Noah had invested his life savings in to help keep Caleb from gambling away the money Noah's parents had left him and get his life back on track, only to have Caleb mismanage it so badly, it might cost Noah his higher level security clearance.

If Anne was phoning him now, before seven in the morning, after almost a year of estrangement, it had to be urgent. He needed to take the call. Just not immediately.

One emergency at a time. Noah breathed a prayer that Caleb, Anne and the kids were safe, and then declined the call.

A light switched on below him and suddenly the space where Holly sat was bathed in a pool of light, but he still couldn't see past the large man blocking his view of her face. Noah stepped closer to the railing. A cable came into view, then a tripod and finally a video camera that the Ghoul seemed to be fiddling with.

Dread surged up inside Noah's core like a geyser. He steeled himself and stepped to the very edge of the catwalk. A second figure in police uniform came into view, this one slender and smaller, sitting at a folding table with a laptop in front of him. Noah guessed that would be the Wraith. Then, as he watched, the hulking form between him and Holly stepped aside and for one long moment revealed her face again. Holly's eyes looked up, directly at Noah, seeming to latch onto his gaze just as directly as they had earlier that morning in front of the safe house.

She knew he was there.

He wasn't sure how well she could see his features at this distance, or if she had any idea that he was there to help her. But he felt the need to let her know that she could trust him, that he was safe, had her back and would help her—even if he still didn't know how. He flashed her a quick thumbs-up and smiled. A goofy gesture, maybe, but one he hoped would let her know he was on her side. She nodded ever so slightly in response. Her eyes were on his face, keen and intent, as if they were asking him a question. They were asking him for something, and he knew that no matter what, he wasn't going to let her down.

He nodded back. *Yeah, Holly, I'm here. I'm on your side. And with God's help we're going to get out of here alive.*

The faintest glimmer of a grin crossed Holly's lips. Then she shouted, "Hey! Who's that behind you on the catwalk?"

Holly had told her kidnappers he was there? Why? What reason could she possibly have for tipping them off and blowing his cover? The Ghoul glanced back toward Noah, skeptically at first, but his eyes quickly widening as he realized someone actually was there. *Yeah, me.* The Wraith slammed the laptop closed and took off running into the rows of boxes and shipping pallets. The Ghoul yanked a gun from his belt, raised his weapon and fixed Noah in his sights.

Holly struck before the thug could fire, leaping to her feet like a fury and spinning, swinging the folding chair around behind her like a weapon. The metal legs caught the criminal in the back of his knees and sent him stumbling forward onto the ground. The gun misfired, and the bullet flew somewhere high above their heads.

Had Holly really been so confident in her ability to disarm the criminal before he could get off a shot that she'd taken the risk of using Noah as a diversion? And a "hey, look behind you!" trick at that? The Ghoul turned back and lunged for her. But Holly was ready for him, with a swift roundhouse kick that sent him stumbling to the floor and the gun flying from his hands. Noah's heart jolted as if someone had just sent an electric current shooting through it. She was fighting back, against an armed kidnapper, with her hands still tied to a chair, even as he could see her strength and energy flagging.

Noah was beyond shocked. He was even beyond impressed.

Above all, he was determined that she wouldn't fight alone. The metal catwalk stretched out on either side of him. Staircases descended into the warehouse at opposite ends. It would take him too long to reach either one, and Holly had been alone without backup long enough.

He vaulted over the railing and let his body drop down into the boxes below.

Holly watched from the corner of her eye as the man on the catwalk dropped out of sight into the piles of boxes. Was she right? Had it been Detective Noah Wilder? She didn't know for sure. But friend or foe, he'd been a distraction she could use to draw enemy attention while she fought for her survival. And thankfully, she'd disarmed the bigger of the two criminals before he could fire at him.

But now what? Pain still pounded through her head and seemed to radiate through her body. The headache was steadily growing worse. She stumbled forward, feeling the weight of the chair straining her arms and nearly yanking her shoulders out of their sockets. The apparently fake police officer who'd kidnapped her lunged at her once more. She swung the chair around again hard, using the metal frame attached to her wrists as both a weapon and a shield. It made impact, she heard a crack and then—thank God—the weight of the chair fell from her arms as the bottom of the metal frame gave way. She shook herself free.

Okay, her hands were still tied, but at least she'd gotten rid of the chair. Now what?

The dull, worrying ache in her skull was like nothing she'd ever felt before and seemed to radiate through her mind, clouding her ability to think. The big guy was down on the ground now, but even though she'd gotten in a few good blows, she didn't expect him to stay there for long. The small guy was nowhere to be seen. She spun back, and the room began to spin with her, sliding in and out of focus like a scene from an old-fashioned projector movie that wasn't sitting right in its frame.

Something was very wrong. *Help me, God!* Prayers beat like a drum through Holly's aching mind. She had to get out of there. She ran, darting down the closest aisle in the maze of towering pallets. Shipping containers and plastic-wrapped boxes rose around her, seeming to wave and move as she passed, like seaweed shimmering underwater. She pressed on, looking for an exit and pushing herself deeper into the labyrinthine maze, hearing her kidnappers pelting down the rows behind her, growing closer with every step.

Too late, she saw a man leap down in front of her. He landed in a crouching position, on the balls of his feet. Then he unfurled to his full height, filling the space ahead of her and blocking her way. She was trapped. She couldn't turn around. There was nowhere to run. The only way out was through.

The man in front of her raised his hands, and all her mind could focus on was that there was a gun in his right one. She didn't wait to give him the opportunity to point it at her. Holly squared her shoulders, lowered her head and ran right at him, like he was nothing but a tackling dummy back in basic training. *Help me, Lord!*

"Corporal Asher!" His voice, deep and warm, spoke her name. "Holly!"

Detective Noah Wilder? She knew his voice. How did he know her real name? But it was too late for her to stop. She crashed into him, keeping her head low and her body strong. But instead of knocking him out of the way, she felt his arms part, as if to catch and receive her. She landed against his chest and he wrapped his arms around her. They tumbled onto the ground, with him on his back and her on top of him, her hands still tied behind her.

Two sets of footsteps were coming toward them now.

"I'm sorry," Noah started. "Are you hurt?"

Sorry for what? Startling her? Catching her?

"You with them?" she asked.

"No—"

"Then let's get out of here before they kill us."

"Hang on." He didn't even hesitate. "We're going to roll."

Hang on how? And to what? He holstered his gun, tucked her head into the crook of his neck and lowered his own head over hers. His arms clasped tighter and then he rolled, taking her with him and sliding their bodies under the shelter of a thick blue tarp covering a pallet nearby. Footsteps and voices grew closer. He yanked the tarp down, covering them like the flap of a tent.

"You're Wilder, right?" she whispered into his ear.

"Yeah. But I told you to call me Noah." His voice seemed to surround her in the darkness. "I'm an RCMP detective specializing in witness protection, and I'm here to get you out of this alive." *Got it.* "Is it okay if I call you Holly?"

"Sure." Right now that was the least of her worries. Her kidnappers grew closer, until she heard them pass just inches away from where they hid.

"Where did she go?" The man's voice was thin, whiny and matched his slight frame.

"I don't know!" the larger one snapped back.

"She saw our faces! She can identify us! We can't let her out of here alive!"

THREE

They were right that she'd seen her kidnappers' faces, and yet, as the pain pounded through her brain, somehow she couldn't seem to draw a clear picture of them in her mind. She held her breath and prayed silently as the sound of their footsteps faded into the distance. Then she turned her attention back to the strong man who was lying beside her and still holding her in his arms.

"Don't worry," Noah whispered. "I've got you."

Had he now? Did that mean he had any idea what was going on and how they were going to make it out alive?

"Now," Noah added, "if it's okay with you, I'd like you to roll over onto your other side so I can check your wrists and untie your hands."

He loosened his hold on her body and she rolled away from him. Her head was hurting less now that she was lying down and the world had gotten quieter. The headache was probably nothing and she'd be fine just as soon as she rested.

She felt his fingers move against her wrists. "Hang on… Did you actually ask permission to free my hands?"

"Not a big fan of touching someone who might be

upset without asking first," he said. "Well, anyone, really. Now, I'm going to use my knife, okay?"

"Go for it." She listened. She couldn't hear her kidnappers' footsteps or voices anymore, but that didn't mean they'd gone far.

"Who are they?" she whispered. "Why were they dressed as cops?"

"They're cyber terrorists," Noah said, also keeping his voice low. "They're called the Imposters. Two-man crew. Big one goes by the handle the Ghoul. The hacker is the Wraith. Really big on staying in the shadows and not being identified. They tend to disguise themselves as law enforcement or emergency services personnel to infiltrate places without being detected. They also kidnap innocent people to do their online missives for them, which I'm guessing is why they set you up in front of the camera."

Well, that would explain why she'd ended up tied to a chair with a camera in her face.

"Why did they target me?" she asked. "Why did they kill Elias? Does this have something to do with my testifying to the inquiry against General Bertie Frey?"

Her hands fell free. She rolled back toward him.

"I really don't know." Noah lifted the tarp a couple inches, enough to let a little light seep through. He was more handsome up close than she'd expected him to be. He had that slightly rugged look of a man who was over thirty and had seen his fair share of battles. His hair was dirty blond, with a short and slightly rumpled cut that, despite his age, made her think of a fresh recruit, and somehow matched the politeness of his tone. "Once I'm sure they're gone, I'll get you out of here to safety.

We can regroup and reevaluate from there, as well as get you medical attention."

"I'm okay," she said reflexively. "I don't need medical attention."

She just needed her head to stop pounding.

"Why were you outside the safe house this morning?" she asked. "And why did you follow Elias's car?"

The niggling in the back of her mind told her there was something else Elias had told her about Noah that she should probably ask about. But her memory of the whole past hour was a little fuzzy.

"According to one of my informants, there'd been some bad internet chatter overnight about the Imposters targeting your route this morning."

"But why?" she pressed.

"Like I said, I don't know."

She suspected Mr. Polite Detective wasn't used to having rapid-fire questions thrown at him, but now was no time for waffling. They were hidden and whispering in their impromptu foxhole, but they couldn't stay there forever. Before she made a tactical move, she was going to learn all she could about the situation they were facing.

And the man who'd leaped to her rescue.

"Did they tell you anything?" he asked. "Do you know what they'd wanted you to read?"

"No." She frowned. They hadn't said much at all. "But I was left with the distinct impression they hadn't been planning on leaving me alive when they were done with me."

His eyes widened. They were gray like the sky before a winter's storm. She watched as a question floated there.

"What?" she asked.

"You turned down witness protection repeatedly," he said. "Why?"

"Because I love my life in the military, I love serving my country and didn't want to give it up. Even temporarily."

Her frown deepened. But to her surprise he grinned. His smile was warm, cheerful and oddly comforting.

"Now, just in case you were worried, I want to reassure you that I really am a cop," he said. "Not that I have any way of proving it to you right now, besides flashing my badge."

To her surprise, she felt a smile curve at the corner of her lips. "It's okay. I trust you on that."

"Good." He lifted the edge of the tarp slowly. "Fortunately, I got a pretty good look at the layout of this place when I was up on the catwalk. So here's the plan. We get somewhere safe, talk to people I trust, figure out what's going on and make a plan from there."

She appreciated that he'd said "we" and not "I."

"Well then," she said, "let's go."

Noah whispered a prayer under his breath. But before she could figure out what she thought about that, he'd pulled the tarp aside and slid out. "Come on!"

She crawled out from under it, leaped to her feet and ran after him. Immediately, the headache hit her again, as unexpected as a left hook. Her knees buckled and for a moment she thought she was going to fall.

Noah stopped, turned back and stretched out his hand. "You okay?"

She looked at the palm extended toward her and hesitated.

Come on, Corporal. Just push through the pain.

"I'm fine." She forced herself forward. "Let's go."

Voices sounded in the distance. Her kidnappers were searching the warehouse, no doubt looking for them. She ran on autopilot, pushing her legs to move, one after the other. Noah started jogging, matching his pace with hers. He rounded a tight corner, then stopped at the end of an aisle. A cargo loading bay lay ahead, up a steep ramp that led to a garage-style door. Light seeped through a two-foot gap at the bottom.

"Okay, so we've got a clear line to run from here to there," Noah said. "We'll have to be fast, then when we're outside, we can lose them. Got it?"

His eyes searched her face. They were worried. She didn't like that.

"Yeah, I got it. Let's go."

He ran, and she followed, keeping her head low as they pelted across the empty space and up the steep incline. So far, so good. He reached the garage door first, dropped to the ground and slid through. Then he looked back at her through the gap and waved at her to hurry. She was trying to. But it was like her legs weren't cooperating and the ramp was growing steeper with every step. She stumbled forward, lost her footing and grabbed a metal loading cart for support. It slipped from her fingers and rolled down the ramp, crashing into the pallets below.

"Hey, over there!" the Ghoul shouted.

A bullet flew past her head, followed quickly by a second. She dropped to the ground and began to crawl.

"Holly!" Noah's voice drew her gaze toward the gap beneath the garage door.

"I'm coming!" She gritted her teeth and dragged her body across the floor.

Noah leaned his torso through. "Here! Take my hands!"

She did, grabbing on to both his wrists as he grasped hers. He yanked her through the gap and out into the snow. She lay there on the ground for a moment, feeling cold wind and thick flakes lash against her skin as prayers of thanks rose within her. Unexpected tears rushed to the corners of her eyes. She blinked fiercely, feeling them freeze before they could fall.

"Are you sure you're not hurt?" Noah knelt beside her.

"I'm fine." She gritted her teeth yet again. "I just have a really, really bad headache and it's making me dizzy. It got better briefly when I was lying under the tarp. I just need to rest quietly for a few minutes somewhere until it goes away."

She pulled herself up to her feet. Sirens sounded around her, echoing off the buildings and surrounding her with noise. Her knees buckled.

"Let me carry you," Noah said.

"I told you, I'm fine—"

"Corporal!" His voice rose. "If you were on the battlefield and a fellow soldier was too dizzy to keep up, would you carry them?"

"If the situation warranted it." Her chin rose. "And for the record, if need be, I'd carry you."

"I don't doubt it," he said. "Now, please let me help you."

"Fine."

She felt one hand slide beneath her knees then and the other along her back, as Noah swept her up into his arms, cradled her to his chest and ran. He dashed through the snow, weaving quickly down back alleys, away from the warehouse, emergency vehicle sirens and flashing lights. Then stopped suddenly in front of a plain, unmarked metal door, where he pressed a button on the speaker box.

"It's me," he said. "I've got Holly. Let me in!"

The device beside the door looked broken and stayed silent. Then it hissed quietly.

"Look," Noah added, "I know you can see me, and I know you can hear me. I promise there are no Imposters on my tail. Let me in. Now!"

The door finally opened. A man stood there, slender and good-looking, in an intense and scraggly way. His blond hair was down to his shoulders and his jaw needed a shave. He narrowed his eyes. "You decided to bring her here?"

"Holly Asher," Noah said, "meet Seth Miles, Canada's most notorious hacker."

"Hi." Holly waved briefly in greeting. Then she glanced at Noah. "I think you can let me down now. Unless we're going to keep running."

Noah put her down carefully. They stepped through the door and Seth closed and locked it behind them. Then he turned to Holly.

"Corporal Holly Asher," Seth said, as he reached for her hand. "I can't tell you how big an honor it is to meet you. I have huge respect for what you've done in risking your career to speak out against a superior officer. I have all the admiration in the world for anyone who stands up to authority and abuse of power. If there's anything I can do to help you, I will."

She shook his hand. "Thank you," she replied. "But I'd like to think I just did what anyone in my position would do."

"You'd like to think." Seth shook his head, then turned back to Noah. "So, witnesses are expected to just double up on safe houses now?"

Noah rolled his eyes and didn't answer.

"I don't want to put Seth in danger," Holly said. "Can't they track us here via security cameras?"

"Not if I've already knocked out all the security cameras in the area and replaced them with dummy feed," Seth said. "I'll also doctor the footage to look like you guys ran north, not south. I'm not saying it's foolproof, but them finding you here definitely wouldn't happen fast and would take a whole lot of fishing. You'll be long gone before they think to check this block."

He flipped open a panel in a wall, revealing a keypad, and pressed in a code.

"I don't remember installing that," Noah said.

It was Seth's turn to snort. He started up a narrow stairway to the top floor of the building, with Holly after him and Noah taking up the rear.

"I gather from the sirens outside that all imaginable emergency services have arrived at the crash site?" Noah asked.

"They have," Seth said. "Bad news is I can't guarantee who out there is the real deal and who's an Imposter. Tell me you saw the Ghoul and the Wraith."

"Not up close," Noah said. "I never saw their faces. But I can tell you that one's big, one's thin and I'm pretty sure both are men."

"Helpful," Seth said.

"Holly got a lot closer to them that I did," Noah added. He waited for her to jump in and agree with him, but she didn't. "Are you any closer to determining if there's a leak in the RCMP?"

"Not quite," Seth said. "But I did pinpoint the person who gave the Imposters Elias's route today and told them how to target him."

"Do we have a name?" Noah asked.

"No, just a handle. Snitch5751."

"Any idea who that could be?"

"Someone with high level security clearance," Seth said, "and current access to a law enforcement or military server. That's all I've got for now."

Well, that narrowed it down. Noah and Holly stepped into the wide and brightly lit loft. Tall windows ran from floor to ceiling on one side, with rough redbrick on the other three. The furniture consisted of a couch, two overstuffed chairs and a coffee table that looked like it had once been a door. A futon bed sat high on a platform by one wall, accessible by a ladder. Not a single computer was in sight.

Holly walked over to the couch and sat down. Seth looked down at her and crossed his arms.

"You actually tangled with the Imposters and lived to talk about it," he stated. "Any idea what they wanted or why they targeted you?"

"None," Holly replied. "It's possible their real target was Officer Crane, and I just happened to be the person he was transporting. I don't think he thought much of the assignment."

"Elias was past retirement," Noah said. "He could pick and choose what assignments he took. I think he requested your case personally."

"Did they get you to read something on camera?" Seth asked.

"They tried," she said. "But they didn't succeed. And no, I didn't see what it was."

"What would happen, hypothetically, if someone managed to see one of their faces and could identify them?" Noah asked.

"They wouldn't stop coming after them until they were dead," Seth said, and Noah felt a shudder run down his spine. "But that still doesn't explain why your transfer into witness protection was targeted. They don't risk coming out of the shadows unless it's a really big job. We're talking huge. Bigger than big. I mean, that inquiry you're testifying at is a big deal for General Bertie's career, but if he could pay big bucks to have you killed, it's unlikely he'd hire cyber terrorists for the job. Hit men have got to be way cheaper than what the Imposters would charge. And it's not like either you or Elias was in possession of something worth millions. No offense."

"None taken." Holly lay back against the pillows and closed her eyes. Her face was way too pale for Noah's liking.

"I still think you should talk to a doctor," he said.

"I don't," Holly retorted. "It's just a headache. I'll be fine in a moment. Seth? Have the Imposters ever impersonated medical personnel?"

"Yup, all the time," he answered. "It's one of their main go-to methods for kidnapping, killing or poisoning people. They've been paramedics, nurses, doctors and other hospital staff."

Was Holly trying to make a point about not wanting to see a doctor? Either way, she'd succeeded in making Noah think twice about just rolling up to a hospital. He looked around the loft, surprised at how hard he found it to drag his eyes away from Holly. "Where are you hiding your computer? Clearly, you have one. Otherwise you wouldn't have tipped me off." Not that he much liked knowing someone he was supposed to be protecting had violated the rules of his agreement.

Seth walked over to a bookshelf and pulled. It swung back on hinges. A neat folding table complete with three monitors and two towers sat inside. One of the screens was cracked and one of the computer towers seemed to be held together by duct tape. Noah noticed the machines were already humming.

"You know the more secrets you keep from me the harder it is for me to protect you," Noah said. He'd have to report Seth for this, but that could wait until after they got to the bottom of whether someone within the RCMP was Snitch5751. "I don't even want to know how you put this together."

"Dumpster diving," Seth said, and sat down at the machines. "It's amazing what you can do with what other people leave behind. Also, I want the record to show that I'm acting as an informant and that I revealed all this to you voluntarily, knowing the RCMP can confiscate it for violating the terms of my agreement."

"Yup, so noted," Noah said. Not that it would necessarily make much of a difference. "Did you manage to get through to Liam, Jessica and Mack?"

The hacker nodded. "They're all on standby a few blocks away."

"Good," Noah said. "Tell them to come here. We'll regroup and figure out what's going on together."

Thankfully, from what Seth had said, it sounded like none of them could be Snitch5751.

"Why not?" Seth shrugged. "I've already got one cop in my loft. Why not make it four?"

"And a corporal," Holly added, her eyes still closed. "And considering your background, I figured you'd hate military more than cops."

Seth glanced back at her over his shoulder, a surprisingly soft smile on his face, and Noah was reminded that the man's first major target was taking down the corrupt military general father who'd abused him.

Yeah, he was probably really happy to be back to taking down criminals online. Noah couldn't imagine how hard it would be for someone like Seth to be cooped up here, in witness protection, unable to do the one thing that made him feel the most alive.

"With your permission, Holly, I'd like to plant some false information about you online," Seth said. "Just some minor red herring stuff so that the Imposters have a harder time finding you."

"Go for it," Holly said.

Seth turned back to the computer, and his grin spread. "Right, I'm going to have you applying for a wedding license in Ottawa, booking a flight from Montreal to London and renting an apartment in Vancouver."

"Sounds like my doppelgänger is having a lot more

fun than I am," Holly said. "Who have you got me marrying?"

"John Smith," Seth said. "It was the most generic fake name I could think of."

Noah's phone buzzed in his pocket. He glanced at the screen. Anne was calling again. He hesitated so long the call went through to voice mail, and then he turned to Holly.

"Listen," he said. "I know a doctor. She's a small-town family physician and she's like a sister to me. How about you just talk to her on the phone and describe your symptoms? If she agrees you're fine, I'll stop pushing you to get medical help."

"And what if she's compromised?" Holly asked. "Or the Imposters are able to hack her line?"

Noah suspected the question was more about wanting to avoid talking to a doctor than worrying about her safety. But Seth spun around on his chair to answer.

"Let me explain how a criminal duo like the Imposters works," he stated. "They're smart and that means being focused. They're not tapping the phones of everybody all across the country. They're looking for anyone the slightest bit related to 'Corporal Hildegard Asher.' They're setting up online traces and snares to catch anything you post or that's written about you. They're looking into your family, your friends, people you've worked alongside and served with. They're turning your life inside out, and since Snitch5751 only told them yesterday that Elias was assigned to transport you, they haven't been at it that long, which makes it the perfect time for me to muddy the waters with fake information, as well. Sure, if they figure out you're with Noah, they'll start digging into his life, too. But the estranged wife of the former foster brother of a detective they probably haven't identified yet isn't anywhere near their radar." He spun back. "Besides, I already have traces running for Noah and the people who matter to him. Of course I ensured her line is secure."

He went back to typing.

Holly opened her eyes and sat up, as if a new thought had suddenly hit her. She looked at Noah. "Seth just said they'd be looking for Hildegard Asher. Which makes sense, since only my closest friends call me Holly. So, why did you?"

Noah gestured to Seth. "He told me to."

"So, it's out there online?" she asked.

"Nope." Seth flashed a grin at her over his shoulder. "Fellow army brat. We went to the same school for a year, even though we weren't in the same grade and didn't have any classes together. My brain's always had a pretty big hard drive and the fact that I heard your birthday was on Christmas made you interesting. We've just got to hope that the Imposters are stopped before they dig too deep."

Holly lay back and closed her eyes again. Seth kept typing. Noah's phone began to ring again. It was Anne, and this was the third time she'd tried to reach him. He whispered a prayer under his breath and answered.

"Hey, Anne," he said. "What's up? Is everything okay?"

"Noah, hi!" The doctor's voice was anxious, but not panicked. "Do you have a minute? I just wanted to talk to you about Caleb and the gym."

That would be Bros Gym, the business he'd invested

his entire inheritance and savings in, alongside the money his parents had generously left Caleb in their will, only to watch his foster brother run it into the ground. And why Noah applying for higher level security clearance would mean investigators poking around all the ins and outs of Caleb's gambling addiction, bad decisions and wreck of a life.

"I've found a buyer," Anne continued. "I can't take living in limbo any longer. Caleb's never here anymore. He doesn't want anything to do with the gym. And our son, Drew, has been accepted to a really prestigious film school program for creature design and special effects, and could use the money from the sale."

Yeah, and untangling his finances from Caleb would get rid of the only impediment to Noah getting a higher security clearance. But it wasn't that simple. It would also mean Caleb getting a sudden windfall of money, thanks to the fact that the inheritance Noah's parents had left Caleb had made up Caleb's share of the investment. And Anne, of all people, knew why that was a very bad idea.

"Hey, Noah?" Seth's voice floated at the edge of his consciousness.

Noah held up a finger. "Just one second."

"It's important," Seth said.

Yes, but so was talking to Anne.

"Just give me one moment."

"No!" Seth's voice rose. "Now."

Noah glanced at him. The hacker's face was as gray as the slush outside.

"Sorry, Anne, I'm just in the middle of something,"

Noah said quickly. "I'll have to call you back." He hung up. "What is it?"

"I figured out what the Imposters were after," Seth said. "Elias's laptop and phone. Somehow they used them to bypass encryption and hack into the RCMP witness protection system's database. My guess is they targeted him because he was the oldest active cop in the program. They might've thought his device would be easiest to hack."

But why hack the witness protection database? The sweeping pile of data was filled with information about the names, locations and identities of hundreds of vulnerable whistle-blowers, witnesses and victims whom the RCMP had hidden and protected over the years.

Noah took three steps toward him, feeling dread drag on him with every one. "Whose secret identity and location were they after?"

"Everyone's," Seth said. "Absolutely everyone. They're putting them up for sale on the dark web. On Christmas Eve, the name, identity and location of everyone in the RCMP witness protection database will be auctioned off online to the highest bidder. We've got six days to stop these criminals, or hundreds of witnesses could die."

FOUR

Fear swept over him. For a moment, Noah stood there, frozen in place, as the full implications of what Seth was saying beat down on him like a hailstorm. The RCMP's witness protection unit was responsible for relocating hundreds of whistle-blowers, former criminals, witnesses and survivors across Canada, giving them new names, lives and identities. These were people Noah and his colleagues were responsible for, including individuals, families and children, many of whom had lived through terrible things. And then risked everything to turn in the criminals they personally knew, putting their own lives on the line for the sake of justice. They'd given up everything—their friends, family, jobs, homes, even their own names and identities—because law enforcement had asked them to, and their own consciences and faith had propelled them to. And because officers like Noah promised to keep them safe. That either the criminals they'd outed or others wanting to discover what they knew might be able to buy their entire file online was horrifying.

This is all my fault... If I'd managed to get Elias to

listen... *If I'd managed to stop the Ghoul and the Wraith in the warehouse, as well as getting Holly to safety...* He felt his limbs shake. *How do I stop this?*

A hand grasped his arm and squeezed slightly. He hadn't even realized Holly had gotten up from the couch, but now she stood behind him, her fingers brushing against his forearm and down along the back of his hand in a gesture that was both reassuring and caring. An unfamiliar warmth spread through him.

"Breathe," she said firmly. "You look like you're about to pass out, and we need your head in the game. It's going to be okay. That's what you told me when we met, right?"

She was a whistle-blower whose life had been threatened and who'd just been kidnapped. He was the witness protection officer. And yet she was reassuring him? But for a moment something about the way she said it almost made him believe her.

"Hey, Noah?" Seth's voice sounded almost like he was being choked. "My name's on the list."

A firm and determined knock sounded on the door below. Holly's touch disappeared from Noah's hand. Instinctively, he stepped between her and the door, sheltering her with his body as he reached for his weapon.

"It's Liam, Jess and Mack," Seth said. He rose, and Noah couldn't help but notice his entire body seemed to be shaking. "The team's all here. I'll go let them in. You figure out what on earth we're going to do."

"Wait!" Noah said. "If the entire witness protection database has been accessed, does that mean they have this address and know that someone in witness protection lives here?"

"I don't think so," Seth said. "I've accessed my file in the past, to scrub my location and replace it with a dummy. They shouldn't know anyone in witness protection lives here. But nothing stays hidden forever. I'll brief them downstairs to give you guys a moment. I'm getting the impression you want one."

Did they? Noah definitely wouldn't mind one. Especially as he had something to ask Holly about that he didn't want to address in front of the rest of the team.

Seth went downstairs. Holly walked back over to the couch and sat down again. Noah sat on the coffee table opposite her, and for a long moment they stayed there, face-to-face, so close their knees were almost touching.

"Don't worry," he said. "Neither Liam, Mack nor Jess can be Snitch5751. They're three of the best people I've ever met, and I trust them with my life."

A niggling in the back of his mind told him that Holly would want to know she was placing her life in the hands of four detectives who weren't on active duty. And he would tell her. It was just a matter of how and when. Or better yet, he'd wait to let them tell her themselves. Their personal stories weren't exactly his to share.

"We have to stop this," Holly said.

We? She was going to stay safe somewhere until the date of the inquiry she was supposed to testify at. He was going to stop this, somehow, with the help of the colleagues Seth was right now letting in downstairs. And to do that, he needed more information than he already had.

"Tell me everything I don't know about this thing you're testifying in," he said. "What do I need to know about General Frey?"

"Bertie," she said quickly. "He tells everyone to call him General Bertie."

She pinched the bridge of her nose and then lay back against the pillows. Her eyes closed again. He heard voices from the stairs. It sounded like Seth was briefing the others in the bottom of the stairwell, and Noah was thankful Seth was giving him and Holly a moment alone.

"It's a parliamentary inquiry," she said. "Which means I'll sit at a table and for days be grilled by government leaders, on camera, broadcast live to the nation, a lot of whom really want to believe that Bertie is innocent and I'm a big fat liar. It could result in his resignation or criminal charges. But if they don't believe me, it could also lead to absolutely nothing but a major setback to my military career."

He noticed she hadn't mentioned leaving the military as an option.

"I've heard about it on the news," Noah said, "and I've read your file. But I'm not going to pretend to understand it. I do know he has a stellar reputation and people really like him."

"He does," she said, "and they do. He was my mentor for years and I felt honored to serve under him on my last tour of duty. Whenever he's home in Canada over the holidays, he throws this huge party at his country estate, in northern Ontario, with elaborate light displays and free turkeys and food hampers for servicemen and -women, and those in other areas of emergency services and law enforcement. Presents for their kids, too. From a sheer military perspective, I loved serving under him. He was a hero of mine." She frowned. "But in my experience people tend to be more complex than you'd think."

He could agree with that. She still hadn't opened her eyes. Just how bad was her headache?

"That part of the world has nomadic tribal families," she continued. "Many live very remotely and have long-standing grudges and rivalries that go back generations. Every now and then violence will break out. It's really horrible and really bad, but it's on a smallish scale."

"I get it," Noah said. "You hurt one of my people, so we hurt one of yours. Like rival gangs in North America. Or something from a historical drama about ancient clans."

"Or Shakespeare," she said wryly. She took a deep breath. "Then suddenly the violence escalated, from knives, sticks and a handful of relatively minor injuries a year, to dozens getting shot by military-grade weapons. About two dozen people were killed at a wedding last year and when local authorities investigated, they found the weaponry came from the Canadian military. Troops on the ground said they'd all been stolen from us."

"But that wasn't true?" Noah asked.

"No." She shook her head, then winced again. "Bertie gave them away. He bartered them, too. He gave weapons to warring families and local warlords so they could 'protect' themselves." Her fingers moved in air quotes. "He did it to build connections. He did it to grease wheels. He did it to gain intel. And whenever I challenged him on it, and believe me I did, he said it was just part of keeping our troops safe and helping us be effective in our mission."

"By arming a handful of local families to increase how badly they could hurt each other," Noah said.

"See, you get it!" Her eyes snapped open. "But to hear most people tell it, I'm the villain here. That's what I'm learning through this. That whether people believe me or not, they still think I'm wrong. The official line is that he's completely innocent. The unofficial line is so what if a few dozen people in a completely different part of the world, who are determined to kill each other anyway, get to it a little faster? Is that worth ruining a good man's reputation and career over?"

The question was rhetorical, but he couldn't have argued with it if he tried. "I get what you're saying. You didn't deserve the backlash, and I'm sorry it drove you into witness protection."

Something flashed hot and fierce in her eyes.

"You think a bit of hate, online chatter and pathetic death threats drove me into witness protection?" she asked. "Nobody and nothing drove me to anything. What happened is three thugs got paid by some unknown fan of Bertie's to jump me in an alley outside base one night, thinking they'd 'teach me a lesson' about 'being quiet and keeping my mouth shut.'"

She'd been attacked? Why hadn't that been in her file? Something tightened in Noah's chest. An unfamiliar pain filled his core. He wanted to protect her. He wanted to defend her. He wanted to step back in time, stop the men who'd tried to hurt her and then stop anyone from hurting her ever again.

"They were caught," she said. "All pled guilty. I don't think investigators have found out who paid them yet."

"But they hurt you," he pressed, gently.

"Not as badly as they wanted to." She shrugged. "I've gone through worse in basic training."

"Yes, okay," he said. "But it had to be serious enough if you went into witness protection..."

"The RCMP and the inquiry officials asked me to go into witness protection because they were worried about losing a witness," she said, "and I felt I had a duty to just go lie low somewhere until the inquiry."

That he believed. He believed she'd have dug her heels in and stood her ground no matter how many random attackers and death threats came at her, and that as much as she seemingly resented being in witness protection, she saw it as some kind of duty.

But none of that changed how much the knowledge that she'd been attacked was tearing him up inside. He'd felt that way growing up sometimes, seeing what his foster siblings had gone through, which had been what had driven him into law enforcement and made him want to dedicate his life to saving people. But the feeling had never quite hit him this fast or this strong.

"Our problem isn't that three random criminals thought they could intimidate me out of doing my duty," Holly continued. "I fought back. I can take care of myself. I always do. What I'm worried about are all those innocent witnesses whose identities are being auctioned off in six days to people who want to hurt them."

There was the sound of footsteps on the stairs, followed by throats being cleared. Noah stood and turned. Liam Bearsmith, Jessica Eddington and Mack Gray stood with Seth at the top of the steps. Noah made brief introductions around the room. Of the undercover detectives, only Liam looked like he could be in law enforcement, but with his broad shoulders and strong jaw he was usually pegged as private security. Most of his undercover assignments were posing as a bodyguard or enforcer for some rich and corrupt man, and he'd helped crack two human trafficking rings. Mack, on the other hand, had an intensity to him, between his jet-black hair, lean strength and sharp blue eyes, that tended to make people think he was either himself a criminal or an actor who'd once played one on television. While Jessica had a diminutive form and bubbly energy that made her come across as a former high school cheerleader whose life goal was to be a soccer mom. All three had faced more guns, investigated more crimes and taken down more violent criminals than anyone would ever guess.

And like him, all three were currently off duty or on leave, for one reason or another.

"What's the situation like outside?" Noah asked.

"Chaotic." Liam spoke for the group. "Tons of emergency vehicles and personnel scrambling everywhere, with no one really knowing what's going on. Several of the empty warehouses have smoke coming out their windows. Emergency response teams are doing a sweep of the area. People don't know if it's a fire, a gas leak or what."

"Are they heading this way?" Noah asked.

"Not yet."

Right. Noah glanced at his watch. He'd give them fifteen minutes, tops, and then they'd have to make a move. "Solutions?"

"Seth briefed us," Liam said, "and here's what we've come up with for a plan. Mack's going to go underground and see what rumblings he can dig up from our various criminal contacts. Jess will head into the witness protection headquarters, right in the office itself for some kind of retraining, and will be our eyes on the inside. Law enforcement will be scrambling to warn witnesses, relocate as many people as possible, as well as find the Imposters. If Snitch5751 is among them, she'll find him or her. Seth will keep doing his thing online. I'm going to go see what I can dig up in the broader law enforcement world, as well as dig into Elias himself. He's been in the force for years. He might've made enemies."

"And one of the red herrings I've posted has already paid off," Seth interjected. "A news organization has already found the fake wedding license application I created and posted it about it on social media. Clearly they had a search running for news about Hildegard Asher. They won't be the only ones. Hopefully the Imposters will chase after my trail of false bread crumbs while I find them for real."

Noah nodded. Absolutely, this all made sense. Which left Noah to keep Holly safe. "So, we fight the battle on five different fronts at once."

"Why not six?" Holly asked. She glanced from Noah to the group of cops and back. "We know they want to find me. As far as we know they've only got two goals right now—the auction next week and killing me. So, why don't we bring them to us? Take me to a new safe house location. Seth can leave a trail of electronic bread crumbs for them to find. We wait for the Imposters to show up and try to kill me. We lay a trap and use me as bait."

* * *

"No." The denial flew from Noah's mouth so automatically he'd barely even paused to let her finish. "Absolutely not."

Indignation welled up inside her. Who was he to tell her what she could and couldn't do? Detective Noah Wilder might have saved her life. He might be strong, kind, competent and not too shabby to look at, either. But he wasn't in charge of her.

"It makes the most sense!" She leaped to her feet. "I've handled way harder and more dangerous missions than this."

But the quick, jerking motion of just rising that fast sent the headache in her skull swelling to a crescendo. Nausea hit her again, this time harder than before. Despite the fact that she'd rested her eyes, the headache seemed to be growing worse. She sat back down.

What was wrong with her? A veteran soldier who'd served her country and taken countless blows in the line of duty was now being sidelined by a headache? She'd taken bad blows before, and she'd always pushed through. She'd trained with bruises, cuts, sprains and even fractures.

Help me, Lord. I'm right about this. I know I am right. Help me get over whatever this pain is. Help me push through. Keep this from stopping me.

She looked up at Noah, just long enough for her gaze to hold his. There was something there, unspoken and invisible, moving through the air between them. She could feel it in the way he was looking at her, the way he was standing almost at attention. The closest thing she could compare it to was that moment she'd look to another soldier on an obstacle course and know without a doubt that if she ever fell, her comrade-at-arms would catch her.

"Don't sideline me, Noah, please," she said. "I'm an asset. Not a liability."

But he shook his head, and she could tell even before he opened his mouth again what the answer was going to be. "No. You can look at mug shot photos and try to identify the Imposters. You can work with a sketch artist to recreate their faces. But I'm not just tossing you out there and hoping they come after you."

His phone began to ring again. It was a loud and raucous rift, which she normally would've liked. But now the noise was so loud it seemed to pierce her skull.

"Is that your doctor friend?" Holly asked. "If so, do you still want me to talk to her? It seemed to really matter to you, and my head is still bugging me."

Noah blinked as if rebooting his mind. Then he nodded. He said a few quick words into the phone that Holly couldn't quite hear, and then handed it to her. "Here you go. I told her your name was Holly, that you were part of a case I was working on and you were in an accident."

She was part of a case he was working on. Well, that was an improvement over being thought of as someone he had to babysit.

"Thank you," Holly said. She leaned back on the couch. Noah hesitated a second, then crossed the room and joined the other detectives by Seth's desk. Their conversation dropped to a murmur. "Hello? I'm…Holly. Thanks for talking to me."

"No problem at all, Holly. I'm Anne." Her voice

was polite and professional. It was warm without being weak. And Holly gravitated to it.

She cupped her hand around the receiver and murmured. "Look. I bumped my head and the headache is like nothing I've ever experienced before. I'm really hoping you're going to tell me I don't have a concussion."

She didn't have days to rest and heal. She needed to be better now. She needed to help join the fight.

There was a pause on the other end of the line and Holly braced herself, waiting for Anne to tell her she couldn't give her a diagnosis over the phone.

Instead she said, "Well, it's possible you do, especially if you bumped your head. But concussions are pretty common injuries and people recover. It's nothing to be afraid of."

She wasn't afraid, was she? She was frustrated. People's lives were in danger and she needed to take action to save them.

"How do you know Noah?" Holly asked.

"My husband was fostered by his family when the two were teenagers," Anne replied. There was a simplicity and directness to her manner. Was it Holly's imagination or had Anne's voice faltered slightly when she'd said "husband"? Holly remembered Seth had said they were estranged. "Noah says you were in some kind of accident?"

"I was." But she was having a hard time remembering it. "A car accident. We lost control and smashed into something. Either a tree or a pole, I think."

"And you hit your head?" Anne pressed.

"I think so," Holly said.

"Do you know where?"

"No," Holly admitted. "The pain's in the back of my skull, but it kind of moves around. Like a halo."

"Can you remember three words for me?" Anne asked. "Tree, ball and dog."

"Yup." That was easy enough.

"Has anyone checked your eyes to see if your pupils look normal and are responding normally?"

"I don't know." But she'd locked eyes with Noah enough he'd surely have noticed if something was wrong.

"Can you touch your finger to your nose, then to your left knee, then back to your nose ten times?" Anne asked.

"Of course." This was ridiculous, but she did it anyway. "Okay, done."

"Now spin your left foot eight times counterclockwise."

She did that, too. "Fine."

"Now what are those three words I asked you to remember?"

Suddenly a picture filled her mind, of her neighbor's backyard as a kid, with his K9 dog lying under a tree chewing a ball. But as she opened her mouth nothing came out. "Dog...and something..." Tears filled her eyes. She closed them tight. "I have a concussion, don't I?"

"I suspect so," Anne said. "I can't diagnose you over the phone, but I suspect you have a traumatic brain injury. A mild one. Along with the headache, you'll probably be nauseous, your brain will be slower than usual and you'll be oversensitive to motion, noise and light. I'd recommend twenty-four to forty-eight hours of complete rest, as soon as you're able, in total darkness to let your brain start to heal. After that, ease back slowly into life."

No, this couldn't be happening. She didn't have time for this. Anne had to be wrong.

"You're also going to want to have someone watching over you," she added, "to keep an eye on your symptoms. And again, see a doctor."

"But I can't afford to have a concussion." Holly wasn't sure if she was saying the words to herself or to Anne, or if she'd even meant to say them out loud. "People's lives are in danger."

"I'm sorry," Anne said. "But if you have a concussion, there's not much you can do about it but rest, take care of yourself and wait."

But how could she? They were counting on her to help them identify the Imposters. They needed her to help stop the auction and save those witnesses' lives. She couldn't let them down.

"Is it possible for me to have a concussion and for the people around me not to know?" Holly asked.

"Yeah," Anne said, hesitating on the word as she said it. "It's very common actually for someone to have a concussion and for those around them not to realize it. They'd probably just think you're confused or tired."

Okay, and she might not even have a concussion.

"But I would also highly recommend you tell Noah and whoever else you're with as soon as possible." Anne's tone sharpened. "You're doing yourself no favors by hiding it."

Holly glanced over to Noah. He was standing with

his back to the window, framed by the swirling snow and pale Lake Ontario waters outside. He looked handsome and strong, in that fresh-recruit way, but also tired and worried. He looked like a man who didn't sleep as much as he should and tried his best to hide it. Above all, he looked utterly reliable and dependable. Like the kind of man who shoveled out the driveway of every elderly neighbor's home on the block and would drive all night through a snowstorm before he let a friend down.

She wasn't going to worry him with this. Not until she knew for sure and not while she could just fight through it.

He glanced her way, his eyebrows lifting. She cupped her hand around her mouth so he couldn't read her lips.

"I have some memory gaps around the accident," Holly admitted. "Some are really sharp." Like the sound of the Wraith's and the Ghoul's voices. "But others, like people's faces, are somewhere between fuzzy and a blank. How long will it take for my memories to come back?"

"I don't know," Anne said. "Could be hours, days or months. Or they might never come back."

Noah was still looking at her. *What do I tell him?*

"But it's also possible I don't have a concussion," Holly pressed.

"Very possible," Anne said. "You might take a few painkillers and be better in an hour."

Okay then. This she liked better.

"But if you do have a concussion, I can't tell you how important it is that you see a doctor and rest," Anne added. "You might feel fine. It might feel like it's not that bad and you're able to push through it. But the harder you push yourself, and the longer you put off resting, the worse the symptoms are going to get."

A crash sounded and the floor-to-ceiling window behind Noah exploded in a spray of glass.

FIVE

"Everybody down!" Noah heard his own voice boom through the loft, rising above the sound of the glass even as it rained down around him. He threw himself forward, just as Holly tumbled from the couch. He caught her, wrapping his arms around her and pulling her to the floor, knocking the coffee table up in front of them like a shield. It was a smoke bomb, nonlethal yet painful. He could tell that much by the acrid smell and the harsh burn in the back of his throat. For a second, all he could hear was the ragged breathing of the rest of the team as they hit the floor, coughing and spluttering. Cold wind whipped into the loft, freezing his skin, but helping disperse the smoke. He watched as Holly pulled herself from his arms and crouched low.

"They're trying to smoke us out," he shouted.

"Agreed!" Liam's voice echoed from the other side of the room.

"Do you think they know we're here?" Jess's voice came through the fog.

"My guess is no," Noah answered. "I think they've narrowed down their options and are probably just fishing." Just at a much faster rate than Seth had predicted. "We've got to stay low."

"No!" Seth called. "We've got to head up!"

"It's a gas!" Mack barked. "Gases rise!"

"But we're in a loft!" Seth was already crawling across the floor toward the ladder. "There's fresh air and a way to get up to the roof!"

Was there? The building didn't have a fire escape or balconies, and Noah was pretty certain he'd have noticed a door to the roof. He glanced at Holly, who shrugged. "Well, it's not what they'd be expecting us to do, right?" she murmured.

True. "Are you okay to crawl, though?" Noah asked. "How about climbing?"

"I don't think we have a choice," she said.

Fair enough. Smoke was filling the air. His colleagues were creeping past them, single file, following Seth's lead.

"Just promise me that if I slip you've got my back," she added.

"Always."

She turned and started crawling, joining his colleagues as they crossed the floor. She reached the ladder and started climbing. He swallowed a breath and stood, his arms raised to catch her if she fell. Another crash sounded behind them as a second smoke bomb entered the room. It detonated. The haze grew thicker, until he could barely see a few inches above his head.

"Holly!" Mack's voice floated from somewhere above Noah. "Here, grab my hand!"

Then he watched her feet disappear from view and heard her body land on the platform above. He grabbed hold of the ladder and climbed up after her, feeling the stinging pain of smoke sear his lungs as he battled the urge to breathe. He forced himself upward, rung after rung, until he reached the wooden platform that served as Seth's sleeping area. Noah crouched there, feeling his head touch the ceiling when he tried to stand. For a second, he was lost, alone in the smoke. Then he felt a large, strong hand grab his shoulder and yank him upward and to the right. He rose and found himself standing inside a ceiling vent. Mack lay on his stomach in front of him. Behind his fellow cop, Noah could vaguely see Holly crawling away.

"This way," Mack said. "It's pretty tight, but thankfully, it's short and widens ahead."

And where exactly was he going? Noah climbed up into the vent and inched along it on this stomach a few feet, before he emerged in a long, narrow, triangular room with sloping windows. Panes that Liam and Jess were in the process of forcing open. An extra-large backpack, a laptop bag and a small cooler sat against the wall, all suspiciously free of dust.

He closed the vent behind him and Mack handed him a wide piece of board to slide over it, blocking any last wisp of smoke. The window opened and fresh wintry air rushed in, clearing the room.

Noah glanced at Seth. "So, when were you going to tell me you had a secret escape route? You didn't think that would be a helpful thing for your witness protection officer to know?"

Seth didn't meet his eye. Noah wasn't really surprised. It wasn't shocking that Seth had trust issues. The brutal mistreatment he'd suffered at the hands of his powerful father had led him to a life in the shadows, with a deep distrust of anyone in authority. And although he seemed to have turned everything around, Noah also had no illusions about the fact that Seth had lashed out as a teenager and briefly tried being the biggest bully in the room, before he'd realized the only place he would ever feel safe was alone. Most people Noah met in witness protection were survivors. Most kids his parents had fostered, too.

It was up to him to give people hope that they could break the cycle. And now, if he and his team didn't stop the identities auction, the very people they'd pledged to protect would be hunted by the same monsters they'd entered witness protection to escape.

Seth still wasn't meeting his eye. "I downloaded the blueprints, discovered this space existed and changed the vents around."

But if you hide things from me, it makes it harder for me to help you. The words crossed Noah's mind, but he didn't speak them. Seth had lost everything at least once before, and now, because he'd tipped Noah off about the Imposters, he would be losing everything again.

Worried faces surrounded him on either side, coupled with tense bodies at the ready, and Noah realized that whether he'd intended to be in charge of this chaotic mess or not, people were now looking at him. All except Holly. She was lying on her back with her eyes closed, almost as if she were trying to nap.

"I think everyone's plan is still a go," Noah said. "Assuming we can find a way out of here. I'm not sure if they're planning on breaching the building or waiting for us to come out. Either way, anyone in uniform who's either bulked up and over six feet tall or looks skinny enough to wash down a storm drain could be an Imposter."

His colleagues nodded. He heard tapping. Seth had a small tablet of some sort in his hands. Noah imagined he had some kind of self-destruct system set up for the computers downstairs.

"Any idea how they found us?" he asked.

"Not from security camera footage of the area," Seth said. "That was clean. But when I accessed the auction, they traced my location somehow. Looks like they're gathering data on everyone who registers to bid. I can create a new dummy account to monitor the auction from, but it'll take me some time."

"Any idea why they're waiting until Christmas Eve?" Jess asked.

"They just accessed Elias's devices an hour ago," Seth pointed out. "Downloading, managing and packaging the data for sale takes time. Then there's advertising, signing up bidders and building hype..."

Noah shuddered. It was evil and vile, but at least it bought them close to a week.

"It's not like you to leave bread crumbs," he said.

"Everyone and everything leaves bread crumbs," Seth replied. "Though most are too small to see and most people aren't savvy enough to find mine, unless I want them, too."

Got it. "You said there's a way out of here?"

"Yeah." Seth nodded. "Through the window, along the ledge until you reach the end, then there are some rough bricks sticking out you can use to climb up. This side of the building faces the lake, so there's a lot less risk of being seen by the crowd now gathering in the street. Then it's just a matter of running and jumping across a few roofs until you hit either a fire escape or stairs down. I've tried out a few routes just for fun. Never in weather like this."

At least the pelting snow would make for decent cover.

"Does that sound like something you're able to do, Holly?" Noah asked.

"Of course." Her eyes snapped open and she sat up. "If Seth can do it, I'm sure I can."

Fair enough, but Seth didn't have her headache. Noah scanned the faces of his colleagues. "Our top priority right now is keeping Seth and Holly safe. There's an empty and highly secure safe house just on the outskirts of Brampton. I suggest we scramble now and meet up again there in an hour."

"Sounds good," Liam said. "I'll take Seth. My truck is hidden in a garage just west of here."

"Someone should go out the front," Mack said, "to make them think they've succeeded in smoking us out. Noah, you can take my truck. It's in a garage by the water. You'll find spare license plates under the front seat, plus a gun in a box under the false floor in the back."

"Thanks." Noah smacked his friend on the shoulder, then gave him a half hug.

"No problem," Mack said. "Just get Holly to safety."

"Will do." Noah ran his hand over the back of his neck. At least everyone had kept their boots and coats on.

"I'll go with Mack," Jess offered. "I actually really liked Holly's bait idea. But let's make it a bait and switch. I'll change jackets with you, Holly. Noah, you and Mack switch jackets, as well. We'll run out the front and make a dash for it. Buy you some cover."

Mack nodded. "That works."

Noah didn't much like the idea of his two colleagues charging through the smoke into a potential ambush. Then again, if the tables were turned, he'd have done the same for them. And he had not a sliver of a doubt they were tough enough and skilled enough to handle it.

"Again, thanks," he said. So his buddy Mack was giving up both his truck and his leather jacket then. "I owe you huge for this one."

"No worries." A grin crossed the other man's face. "I know you're good for it."

"Hang on, I got something that might help," Seth said. He rummaged in his rucksack and came up with a short dark wig. Just how much work had he put into his escape plan? Noah wondered, as Seth handed it to Jess. "It's not the best, but from a distance, in this snow it should throw them off a bit."

"Sounds good," Jess said. She twisted her hair up and tugged the wig down over it. Then she shrugged off her coat, as Noah and Mack swapped theirs.

Seth grabbed a jacket from his rucksack and shoved his arms through the sleeves as Noah turned to Holly.

"Did you catch that? We're going to scramble and then meet up again in Brampton in an hour."

"Yup, I did." She got it, but something about the look on her face told him she didn't like it.

"Do you still have my phone?" he asked.

"It's in my pocket," she told him. "I ended the call

when the first smoke bomb came through the window."
She pulled herself up onto her knees, slid the phone
from her pocket and handed it to him. Then she tugged
her coat off and swapped it for Jess's. "I need to talk to
you about something."

He glanced around the room. Mack and Jessie were
getting ready to crawl back through the vent. Seth was
halfway out the window.

"Okay, we'll talk once we're out of here and somewhere safe," he said.

"God go with you." Liam clasped his hand on Noah's
shoulder.

Jess and Holly exchanged a quick hug.

"Stay safe," Jess said. She hugged Noah briefly in
turn. "See you soon."

"You, too."

Mack and Jess disappeared through the vent and
into the smoke. Liam and Seth slipped out the window
and made their way along the ledge to the right, leaving Noah and Holly alone.

"We'll give them a two-minute head start and then
we'll go," he suggested. "How's your head?"

"Not great," she confessed. "But lying quietly helped."

He straightened back up to standing, and when Holly
rose in turn, he found himself reaching for her hand.
She took it, grasping his wrist with her fingertips. They
stood there face-to-face in the narrow space, while the
cold wind and snow whipped at them through the window. Then her hand slid slowly from his. The frown
lines on her face grew deeper.

"I'm guessing you don't like this plan," he said. "If
it's any help, I don't blame you and probably dislike it

for the same reason. I want to be the one running out there into the melee and opening fire. I don't want to be slinking out the back to safety. I never do. Hey, if it were up to me I'd don a red cape and fly around, single-handedly saving everyone."

A laugh slipped from her lips. "Yeah, I can kind of see that about you."

He chuckled, too, and wasn't quite sure when his arms parted and she stepped into them, but the next thing he knew, he was clasping her with the same kind of camaraderie or foxhole hug he'd given his colleagues just moments before. She hugged him back, hard.

"You know how it is." He tightened his grip around her. "Sometimes you're the one running into danger. And sometimes you're the one ducking, covering or even retreating. In another place and another time, you and I would be the ones out front, drawing fire and letting other people slip out the back."

She relaxed slightly, and it was like she somehow softened in his arms. He felt his palms slide down her back, gently now, until the hug felt nothing like the quick, strong ones he'd given his fellow detectives moments ago. Her hands came to rest behind his shoulders. But still neither of them ended the hug.

"I don't want anyone risking their life for me," she said in a low voice.

He pulled back just enough that he could see her face, and something caught in his chest at how deep both the worry and pain were that floated there. She'd radiated pure defiance and strength when he'd first laid eyes on her. Now something else hovered within their green depths: vulnerability.

"Hey, it's okay," he said. "They're amazing cops and it's a team effort. We'll get you working with a sketch artist and going over mug shots as soon as we hit the Brampton safe house. The two most important things right now are keeping you safe to testify against General Bertie, and stopping the Imposters, and both of those involve keeping you alive."

But still her head was shaking, and he could feel the softness of her pixie cut brushing against his fingertips.

"Look, I get it," he said. "I really do."

"No, you really don't," she said. "I don't think I can identify the Imposters. I can't remember what their faces look like."

I might have a concussion, Noah. I don't know for sure, but your doctor friend suspects I might have a mild traumatic brain injury. She heard the words fill her mind but didn't know how to push them past her lips. She'd never been one for admitting weakness. Sucking things up, forbearance and pushing through was more the way she'd been raised. Her mother hadn't complained about how a military wife's life of moving every few months had meant losing any opportunity at having her own career. And wouldn't have put up with Holly whining that being the only child in a military family meant constantly being the strange new kid in class. The men and women she'd gone through basic training with hadn't fussed about the pain of sore muscles, scrapes or bruises. Besides, she didn't know if Anne was even right. After all, if Holly did have a concussion, wouldn't she be in more pain? She'd been hurt far worse than this dull, persistent ache that felt less like an injury and more like getting up after a night of barely sleeping and having taken cold medication.

"Do you understand what I'm saying?" she asked. "I honestly can't remember their faces right now."

Noah shrugged, and she felt the movement through her body.

"That's pretty common with witnesses and people who experience trauma." His voice was caring and sweet, but neither of those things were what she wanted right now. His fingertips brushed the small of her back and suddenly she was extremely aware of the fact that she was still hugging him. What was she doing? She'd never once fallen into anyone's arms and expected them to save her. She wasn't about to start.

"I wouldn't worry about it," he was saying. "Now, are you okay to climb or do you need me to help you? The ledge isn't that high, but as long as you're able to hold on to my back, I can carry you."

A crash sounded in the distance, once again the sound of breaking glass.

"No, I'm good." She pulled out of his arms and then pressed her hands up against his chest as she pushed him away. The fact that he'd carried her once was embarrassing enough. But she'd rested since then and her head was pounding less now. "I don't need you to baby or coddle me, Detective. I'm a full-grown, adult soldier. Come on. Let's go."

Noah's eyes widened, and she wondered if, despite the fact that she'd tried to sound lighthearted, she'd somehow offended him. Or if something else was going on behind those gray orbs. Then something shifted in his gaze, replacing the confusing softness she'd seen there just moments before with a firmer resolve. He turned and climbed through the window and out onto the ledge.

Holly pulled up the hood of Jess's jacket and fastened it tightly. Then she followed him out the window. The ledge was about a foot wide and three stories off the ground. The blaring sirens were louder now. The flashing lights from emergency vehicles on the other side of the building cast odd red and blue hues in the sky. Thick snow pelted against her, cold air lashed her body and for a moment it was only the relief at how the freezing cold numbed the pain in her skull, and the sheer determination not to fall, that kept her from tumbling backward over the edge. She could do this, right? She'd definitely climbed higher, narrower things before. She reached up and felt the rough groove of a gap between the bricks above her head. She glanced to the side, Noah was already several feet ahead of her.

"It's a tiny bit slippery," he called, "but there are good handholds! Just take it nice and slow. You should be fine."

"Don't worry about me." She gritted her teeth and dug her fingers in deeper. He didn't know that Anne said she might have a concussion. He didn't have to know. "Just go. I'll catch up."

She pressed her body against the rough brick wall and slid her feet and fingertips inch by inch along the ledge. Hopefully, he'd known she'd meant it when she'd said if tables were turned she'd have carried him through the snow to Seth's. If she was back to full strength, she'd have even climbed along this ledge at twice the speed he was going now, with him clinging to her back. If she wasn't injured, she'd have handled all this on her own, without breaking a sweat. And sure, Noah was undeniably strong, brave and also kind of sweet. Definitely the type of man she'd be happy to serve alongside and get to know better. But something about the way he wanted to take care of her irked her. It was like he thought she needed taking care of. Like he thought she was fragile or something, when she'd happily match her wits, strength, skills and mettle against his any day of the week. And beat him half the time.

She kept moving forward, inch after inch, her eyes focusing on the brick so close to her face. She glanced to her right. Noah was gone.

"Noah!" She shouted his name into the wind. "Where are you?"

"Here!" His voice came back to her, strong and solid. She glanced to her right. He'd somehow climbed up onto the roof and was now reaching down toward her. He stretched out both hands. "Grab on! I'll pull you up!"

Except he'd clearly made it up without help. She scanned the wall. A series of uneven bricks jutted out at the edge of the building in what was clearly an intentional pattern. Looked like they'd been recently wiped clear of snow where his hands had grasped them.

She made her way over and started climbing, her toes wedging deep into the grooves. Truth was, she wasn't exactly sure why she was being so stubborn. Was she trying to prove to herself that she didn't have a concussion? To Noah that she was stronger than he apparently thought she was? Or was she simply afraid that if she stopped moving the nausea would sweep over her again?

His hand brushed her shoulder as she neared the top. She yanked herself over the edge and onto the roof, then lay there for a moment, feeling the snow pelt against her. Then she dragged herself up to a crouching position. "Update?"

Noah's eyebrows rose. Then he walked over to the edge of the roof and looked down. She resisted the temptation to do the same. Anne hadn't been wrong when she said Holly would probably be sensitive to motion, noise and light. Heights weren't so great, either.

"I count five buildings with smoke coming out the windows," he said, "and a whole ton of emergency vehicles. We probably won't hear from the rest of the team until we meet up at the safe house. Now, are you good to run?"

"Yeah." Pushing herself back to her feet was harder this time than it had been before. But what other option did she have?

Noah started across the roof. She followed after him, pushing her body as hard as she could, forcing herself to just keep putting one foot in front of the other. She clenched her jaw and leaped after him, nearly stumbling to her knees when she landed safely on the other side. Sirens roared, lights flashed and the smell of smoke filled the air. Every step, breath and heartbeat seemed to hurt worse than the one before.

Her legs were growing weaker. Another gap between two buildings loomed ahead, this one not much wider than the one before. But it might as well have been the length of a football field. *Help me, Lord!* She threw herself across the chasm, praying every second that she'd make it to the other side. Her feet hit the roof and her body collapsed there.

Noah stopped and looked back. His hand hovered at

his side, and part of her willed him to reach for her. She wanted him to grasp her hand, pull her up and help her run. She wanted his support.

Almost as much as she wanted his respect and to prove to him she didn't need it.

"You okay?" he asked.

"Yup. Let's keep going."

She clenched her jaw and rose.

All she had to do was make it to the safe house, where she could close her eyes and lie down. Then she could rest and get up feeling better. It was all she needed to do.

A metal door stood in a small concrete bunker in the middle of the roof. Noah ran toward it and yanked the handle. When it didn't budge, he delivered a swift roundhouse kick to the frame that popped the door off its hinges. He pushed through into a steep and narrow stairwell. "This way. Come on!"

He ran down the steps and she stumbled after him, barely able to keep her feet underneath her as they pounded downward, spiraling floor after floor, until they burst through another door and came out into a small, dingy parking garage with a low ceiling. A battered-looking black pickup truck sat alone against a concrete wall.

Noah pressed a key fob and the truck's headlights flashed. A deep and powerful purr filled the underground space, revealing a far more powerful engine than the vehicle's exterior let on, and she couldn't help but wonder how much Mack was looking forward to being reunited with his truck when they reached the safe house.

There was a hesitation in Noah's step as they crossed the floor, as if he wanted to wait for her or reach for her but didn't know if he should. She paused as he made a tactical sweep of the vehicle, then she climbed in the passenger side while he swapped out the license plates. She leaned back against the seat, closed her eyes and breathed a sigh as he leaped in and put the truck in Drive.

Okay. She'd made it off the ledge, down from the roof and into the safety of the truck. Now all she had to do was lie back and let Noah drive them to the safe house. She felt the vehicle begin to move and heard the sound of a garage door opening and closing. And then the sharp and sudden cold coming through the windows as the truck moved outside.

"Yeah, good idea, stay in your hood and keep your face hidden." Noah's voice hovered on the edges of her consciousness. "There are emergency vehicles everywhere. Then again, I did tell Seth to call in everyone."

The truck came to a stop, she heard the rhythmic noise of the windshield wipers working furiously, then the truck started moving again.

"We'll be there in about an hour," Noah said. "Maybe less. Oh, no…"

"What?" She sat up and opened her eyes.

"We're being followed," he muttered.

She glanced back. A white police cruiser was trailing them, about three car lengths back. She couldn't see the driver's face beneath the hat and bushy beard.

Not to mention he was wearing sunglasses.

"Because everyone needs sunglasses in a snowstorm on a cloudy day," she said.

"Yup," Noah said, through gritted teeth. "Not suspicious at all. You think it's the Ghoul?"

"He definitely has the build for it," she agreed.

Noah pulled off one road and into another, narrower one. A long, empty stretch of Port Lands lay ahead of them. He hit the accelerator and the truck picked up speed.

"So, your plan is to lose him?"

"Well, I'm going to try," he said. "I really don't want him trailing us all the way to the safe house."

He pulled up a ramp and onto the elevated highway. The cop car followed. He gunned the engine and wove between traffic. The cruiser behind flashed its lights and turned on its siren, the sudden cacophony of lights and sound sending a spike of pain through Holly's skull. The truck drove faster. Her head was pounding worse. The Ghoul signaled at them to pull over.

"Not going to happen," Noah said. He reached into his side holster, pulled out his weapon and offered it to her. "Okay, I've got a plan. Judging by your bio, you're an excellent shot. I'm going to pull off the highway onto a hopefully much more empty street near the fairgrounds where the Canadian Exhibition takes place in the summer, and then drop speed. I'll aim for the stretch where the Ferris wheels and bigger rides normally go, south of the soccer stadium. That whole area should be deserted this time of year. When we've got him somewhere more isolated, you'll shoot out one of his tires. Okay? We'll make him spin out, then I'll head back to the highway while you call the crash in with 9-1-1. The goal is the safest possible crash in a deserted area. Got it?"

"Uh-huh." Her chin rose. Would he have asked her to make the shot if he'd known she might have a concussion? Probably not. But that didn't matter. It was a fantastic plan and one she definitely had the skills for. A shot like that she could take with her eyes closed. She checked the gun for bullets, took the safety off and then glanced in the side mirror again. The Ghoul was still on their tail.

She lowered the window and leaned out, looking back as the truck surged forward. Wind whipped her hair and snow lashed her cheek. The vehicle swerved hard to the left and her stomach lurched. It was like going backward on a roller coaster, only much, much worse. The sound of the siren filled her ears and sent pain pounding through her skull. Her vision swam as the flashing lights hit her eyes. Nausea swept over her, churning her stomach and sending her head spinning.

Holly braced her elbow on the window frame and forced herself to focus on the vehicle behind them. Anne had said the symptoms would get worse if she didn't stop and rest. She'd warned Holly that she'd be oversensitive to motion, noise and light. But nothing had prepared her for this.

The truck swerved again. She gritted her teeth. She could do this. She had to. All she had to do was make the shot, stop the Ghoul and then she could close her eyes and rest.

"Now!" Noah shouted. He tore down a deserted strip of road between empty exhibition buildings. The lights and siren were like a barrage beating against her senses. "Fire!"

He yanked the wheel so swiftly that the truck spun.

Help me, God! The gun slipped from her fingers, tumbled through the window and out into the snow. Unconsciousness swept over her. And the last thing she remembered before she passed out was Noah shouting at her to fire.

SIX

"Holly! Corporal! Now!" Noah yelled.

He glanced from the bearded Ghoul in the rearview mirror to the archway signaling the end of the fairgrounds ahead. The plan had worked perfectly so far. Now all it was missing was a bullet. He'd known the plan was beyond risky, to shoot out the tire of a criminal masquerading as a cop in a downtown Toronto street. It would take an expert driver and a sharpshooter. Thankfully, he had one of the best shots in the country on the seat beside him.

"What are you waiting for?" he shouted. "Take the shot!"

Only then did he dart a glance at the soldier beside him. Holly was curled up on the seat with her head slumped against the door, almost like she was sleeping. His heart stopped. She had one arm wrapped around her head. The other fell across her body as if she was trying to shield herself from an unseen or invisible enemy. His gun was nowhere to be seen. And of all the horrors and things Detective Noah Wilder had seen in his life, none had ever scared him quite as much.

He grasped the steering wheel with one hand and reached for her with the other, brushing her neck for the beat of her pulse, and felt the warmth of her breath on his fingers.

Thank You, God! She was still alive and breathing.

The Ghoul's cop car behind him was closer now. The lights were flashing and the siren was blaring. The vehicle lurched forward, ramming into them and slamming its bumper against the truck. Noah grabbed the wheel with both hands and fought to keep it on the road. Holly cried out in pain, and he felt visceral pain shooting through his own body. She wrapped her arm tighter around her head.

"Holly!" His voice rose. His eyes darted rapidly from the car in the rearview mirror to where Holly lay on the seat beside him. "What's going on? Where's my gun?"

"Dropped it." Her voice was muffled. "Sorry."

"Where?"

"Out the window." Her eyes were closed, but her voice sounded pained and exhausted to the point of tears. "I'm really sorry."

"It's okay," he said, not even knowing why he was comforting her. "I'm really sure it's not your fault. And when we're stopped I can grab Mack's gun from the back. But now I've got to do some fancy driving. Just… hold on. Hold on!"

His jaw set. The car behind shot toward them again. The memory of how the last bump had impacted Holly moved through him. No, he wouldn't make her feel that pain again. He shouted at the car's hands-free system to dial Liam. His phone rang, sending rock-and-roll music through the cab.

"Liam!" He shouted his colleague's name the second the phone clicked. "Update!"

"Westbound on the 401 in the collectors." Liam's voice shot back, without so much as a hello. "Seth's safe and well. No sign of trouble."

"Wish I could say the same," Noah said. A big-box hardware store loomed ahead on his left. Thankfully, it was still closed. He cut across the two lanes of traffic and sped through the parking lot, dodging the sole car parked there. Tires screeched as the Ghoul missed the turn. Okay, Noah had bought himself a few seconds, until the Imposter turned around and caught up again. "Going to head east to the DVP, take 404 north and then double back around."

He heard Liam pray and Seth demand to know what was going on.

"And Holly?" Liam asked.

"Injured." It was the simplest answer for now. "Conscious but out of commission."

And in need of a doctor.

He swerved back onto the highway, ignoring the honking of angry drivers and praying with every move he made for the safety of those around him.

He heard another whispered prayer and then, "What do you need?"

"I need this cop car off my tail," Noah said. "Especially before anyone gets hurt or some other emergency vehicles decide to leap into the chase."

Early morning commuters now clogged the road into the city. He prayed the road out would stay empty. Liam and Seth seemed to be arguing, but he wasn't sure about what.

"Tell me the Imposters don't have the ability to mobilize an army of emergency vehicles to close the road ahead," Noah said.

There was a beep.

"Of course they can," Seth said, and Noah realized he was now on speakerphone. "The question is whether or not they would. My guess is no. Too high a risk of being seen. Not much ability to blend into the crowd."

The Ghoul was back behind him now, about three cars away and gaining fast. In a few minutes he'd reach a major junction. Whatever he was going to do, he had to decide by then.

"Give me the make, model, license plate and description of the car," Seth said. "Fingers crossed, its onboard computer is connected to the internet. I'm going to try to triangulate satellite footage against the Imposters' usual internet trails and see if I can access the car's computer."

A slow-moving car loomed ahead. Noah swerved around it. Beside him, Holly stirred and whimpered under her breath. Noah prayed. He could feel sweat building at the back of his neck.

"What'll that do?" Noah asked.

But in a moment he had his answer in the rearview mirror. The siren and lights behind him stopped. Instead, the horn began to honk and the windshield wipers flew. The car slowed.

"I've only bought you a few moments," Seth said. "That's all. It's a pretty light show. No more."

Maybe, but he'd take it. Noah swerved off the highway, darting onto a wide suburban road on his right. Then he cut north, weaving his way through a maze of new subdivision buildings under construction, their snow-and-ice-covered streets deserted in the morning light.

A second call buzzed through on his phone. It was Anne.

The one person who might know what was wrong with Holly.

"I've got to go," Noah said. "I've got another call coming in. Thanks for your help."

"Still on for meeting at the safe house?" Liam asked.

"Hopefully. I'll keep you posted."

"Go with God."

"You, too." Noah glanced in the rearview mirror. He'd managed to buy himself a few more moments, but he still hadn't managed to shake his tail. The road ahead disappeared into a steep, tree-lined slope leading into some woods. He switched the truck into four-wheel drive and prayed Mack had good snow tires. He hit the button and answered the doctor's call. "Anne!"

"Noah!" Her sensible, strict voice filled the truck. "Where are you? Why are you shouting?"

The truck left the road. Then he was driving up and up, into the trees, over dirt and snow. The vehicle jolted. Holly cried out in pain.

"Tell me you're not in a car with Holly right now!" Anne's voice rose.

"A truck, actually." The track disappeared into the woods. Tree branches buffeted the paneling in a series of smacks, thuds and high-pitched squeals as they scraped against the paint. "Outrunning a really bad guy."

Oh, Mack, I owe you big.

"How's Holly?" Anne asked.

"Not good," he said. "Semiconscious."

Anne sighed, the sound loud and exasperated. "What were you thinking, taking her anywhere? She needs to rest!"

"Place she was resting was under threat by bad guys, too," he said. "It's been that kind of day." He glanced at the rearview mirror. No cop car. Nobody following. He gritted his teeth and focused on steering. "What's wrong with her?"

"She didn't tell you?" Worry and even more exasperation filled Anne's voice.

"No, she didn't," he said. Had she tried to? "What don't I know?"

"I can't divulge—"

"Anne!" His voice rose. "She's a witness in a major investigation! She's clearly in pain. She's been in a car accident, she's been kidnapped and now we're on the run. In what until recently was a high-speed chase." Not to mention she'd dropped his gun. "So please, tell me what I need to know to help save her life."

There was a pause, one longer than he liked.

"She thinks I have a concussion," Holly murmured, her eyes still closed. "Little one."

Oh, Anne did, did she? And when was anyone going to tell him this?

"Yes, I think Holly might have a mild traumatic brain injury," Anne said.

What? Yes, he'd realized she had a headache, but he'd never realized she had an actual brain injury! Pain, worry and frustration swelled up inside him like colliding waves. And Holly hadn't told him? And she'd instead climbed out a window and run across rooftops? He glanced at her. She'd shifted position on the seat now and was curled up into an even smaller ball. She looked infuriatingly peaceful, vulnerable and beautiful, with only the crease between her eyes to show the pain she was in.

"Do you really, Holly?" he asked. "Did you actually climb out a window onto a ledge, into a snowstorm, knowing you could have a brain injury?"

Holly nodded. "Just a mild one, though."

She had to be the most infuriatingly driven and stubborn person he'd ever met. She'd told him not to baby or coddle her. She'd pushed his hug away, making him feel foolish and confused about why he'd even been hugging her like that in the first place. So he'd let her take off along a ledge three stories off the ground, climbing walls and jumping rooftops in the snow. And all that time she'd potentially had a far more serious injury than he'd realized.

The trees thinned out ahead, and he found himself on a small rural highway. He drove west, scanning the rearview mirror. He'd lost his tail. The Ghoul was gone.

"Holly. You. Need. Rest!" Anne dropped each word like a gavel. Then her voice softened. "Noah, I'm not shocked that she pushed herself or that you weren't aware of how badly she was injured. The symptoms can be intermittent and mild at first. I've known people who've taken hours or even a day to realize what they actually have is a concussion. And by that point they've made themselves so much worse than they would've been if they'd just rested earlier."

"What do I do?" Noah asked. His eyes scanned Holly's form. She'd gone quiet again, but he assumed she was still listening.

"Holly needs to rest," Anne said. "It's that simple. She just needs lots and lots of rest, in a quiet and dark place, for a couple of days at least, and then after that she can ease herself back into life. Slowly. It might be days before she can safely drive a car or read anything on a computer screen."

Or fight off a villain. Or fire a gun.

Or identify the Imposters' mug shots or work with a sketch artist to help catch the cyber terrorists who were about to sell hundreds of stolen witness protection identities online.

"Got it," he said. *Help me, Lord. What do I do?*

"And it goes without saying, she needs to be seen by a doctor who can actually diagnose her," Anne said.

And there was only one doctor he trusted now, above all others.

He turned north. "I'm bringing her to you."

Noah and Anne's conversation floated around the edges of Holly's consciousness, filtering through the haze of pain. But thankfully, the siren, lights and the painful, unending jolts of the truck climbing through the woods had stopped.

Maybe Anne was right. Maybe she had pushed herself too hard. But that was the only way she'd ever known how to be. Taking it easy was such an anathema she wouldn't know how to do it if she tried. Had she actually made herself worse? Fear rose up inside her, giving her a deeper sense of helplessness than she'd ever felt before.

Help me Lord. I'm feel so scared and so stuck. I've never felt this weak before.

She was never truly stuck. Not for real. There was always a way out, if she just pushed herself hard enough, and made smart decisions. It was a mantra she'd lived by for as long as she could remember, and one that had helped her through everything from changing high schools five times in four years, to surviving basic training, to even dealing with the prospect of testifying against General Bertie in the parliamentary inquiry about the weapons he'd illegally bartered away.

It was how she'd always felt as soon as she was old enough to realize how her beautiful and strong-willed mother had totally given up her life to follow her equally strong and talented father around the world. It had been love at first sight for her parents—at least how her mother told it. When the award-winning horticulturalist had met the dashing soldier home between deployments, it had taken her less than a week to decide it was love, pack up her life and follow him around the globe. And the whirlwind romance had made them happy, for a while, until not having a life of her own had slowly driven her and Holly's dad further and further apart.

Why was Holly thinking about them now?

She opened her eyes, but all she could see was cold and snowy gray, so she closed them again. Somehow, for now, keeping them closed was easier on her head.

"Does this mean we can talk seriously about Caleb and selling the gym?" Anne asked.

Who was Caleb? And what gym?

"Look, I'm not going to promise anything," Noah said, "at all. Except that we can talk. Okay?"

"Deal," Anne said, and it was like Holly could hear an invisible handshake in her voice. "But we are going to talk."

"Heard that," Noah said, and Holly had the distinct impression that whoever Caleb was and whatever the gym situation was about, it was a conversation Noah didn't much want to have. "What can I do to help Holly until I get there?"

"Drive safely," Anne said. "As slowly and carefully as you can. Talk to her, keep her calm and assure her everything's going to be okay. How far out are you?"

"Half an hour," Noah said. "Not even. Maybe twenty minutes."

"I'll have Lizzy's room ready for her," Anne said. "She just turned four and thankfully is already in a full-size bed. Plus Lizzy will be thrilled to have a sleep over in my room."

"We're not going to be staying that long," Noah said. "Just long enough for you to look at her. Then we're going to meet the rest of the team at the safe house."

There was a pause. "But we are going to talk about Caleb," Anne said.

"Yeah, we'll talk."

A few awkward pleasantries later and the call ended. Then Noah phoned first Liam and then Mack and Jess and informed them he was taking a detour but would meet up with them later in the Brampton safe house. Apparently, the Imposters had gone dark and panic was starting to spread through the RCMP ranks about the upcoming auction of the stolen witness protection files.

Those calls ended, too, and a cold, uncomfortable silence spread between them, punctuated only by the rattle of a now loose fender, the purr of the engine and the squeak of the tires on the snowy ground.

Help me, Lord. I've never felt so useless. I hate everything about this. Hundreds of people's lives are in danger. Their lives are about to be auctioned off to criminals intent on hurting them. And there's nothing I can do to stop it.

Desperation filled Holly's core. It was like she'd fallen down a deep dark hole with no light and no way out. What if she never remembered the Imposters' faces?

"So, we're going to Dr. Anne Reed's house," Noah said finally, after a long silence. "It's just outside Keswick. It's a small and really beautiful little community the southern edge of Lake Simcoe. She lives in this tiny farmhouse in the middle of nowhere about a ten minutes' drive from town."

Holly wasn't sure if Noah knew she was listening, if he was following Anne's advice or if he just wanted to break the silence. But there was something comforting about his voice and she held on to the sound like a lifeline.

"Really remote place," he added. "As Seth mentioned back at the loft, once they stop chasing red herrings and figure out you're with me they'll start digging into my entire life. But for now, the estranged wife of my former foster brother isn't anywhere near the top of their hit list. Especially if they haven't identified me yet. Plus, as Seth mentioned, he has a trace running on her so if anything shady pops up he'll let us know, especially once I let him know that's where we're headed."

Yeah, she remembered that.

"The place has got terrific lines of sight," he added. "And the Imposters have always been big on disguises and stealth, so it's not like the two of them are likely to storm a farmhouse. It's not their style. We'll be a lot safer with her than heading to a hospital. Anne can check you out and give her advice, you can rest, we can regroup and then head to the safe house to meet up with the rest of the team."

She tried to nod, but nodding hurt, so instead she murmured something she hoped sounded vaguely affirmative. But she couldn't tell if he could he could hear her over the sound of the truck.

"So, Anne is like a sister to me," he said, after a long moment. "Her kids, Drew and Lizzy, actually call me Uncle Nah, which is short for Uncle No-Nah, because of their dad, Caleb. But she and I aren't related in any way that leaves a paper trail. At least not the kind that anyone who doesn't know me really well would think to look for."

He had no idea how much just the simple sound of his voice mattered to her, to hear something beyond her own panicked thoughts rattling around inside her skull. He likely had no idea she was listening. But there was this quality to his voice. It was very solid and very strong, and something she could hold on to. It was something she could use to get out of this hole.

"Okay, I'm telling this all wrong," Noah said, after another long moment. "I grew up in Alberta. I'm technically an only child—like you, according to your file.

But my parents had been fostering children before I was born. They'd come and live in our home for days, weeks, months, sometimes even years. It all depended on the situation. In one way I'm an only child, but in another I had twenty-two temporary brothers and sisters, growing up."

And she'd had a pretty stable family but moved nineteen times. So it was totally different, and on some level she could relate to the idea of constant change. He paused for a long moment and she found herself missing the sound of his voice.

"Caleb moved in when I was twelve and lived with us until he was nineteen," Noah finally continued. "He was two years older than me, but in a way it was like he was a younger brother. He had a lot of problems with impulse control."

Okay, and where was Caleb now? She could only guess, from the fact that Noah hadn't said anything about seeing him, that he no longer lived with Anne.

"Now, I have no clue what Anne ever saw in him," he said, "or why she's taken him back so very many times. But I always got the impression her home life was really rough. Her father was a real piece of work and for all his other problems Caleb wouldn't even swing at a fly. Anyway, she and Caleb started dating when he was sixteen and she was seventeen. Then they discovered she was pregnant. Eighteen, brilliant, straight-A student, full scholarship to medical school, and pregnant by my high school dropout brother, who'd already been caught twice for shoplifting." He laughed. "I didn't get it. I never have with those two."

"Maybe it's love," Holly said. Like her mom and dad.

The kind of reckless love people lost themselves in. The kind she'd never let herself succumb to.

Even though she'd felt the words slip from her lips, she wasn't sure she'd spoken them out loud until she felt Noah brush his hand across her arm and heard the joy in his voice. "You're awake!"

She tried to nod, then winced.

"Yeah," she said. "Somewhat."

"You should've told me you had a brain injury," he said.

"Potential, mild injury," she corrected. But he wasn't wrong, and she would've if she'd known how badly it was going to hit her. "But I thought I could push through and handle it."

And she had, to an extent, right up until she'd dropped his gun.

There was a longer pause, and she opened her eyes. The sky was pale gray outside, as bright as she imagined the winter's day was going to get. Fields and trees spread in every direction, the emptiness and long expanses of white the exact opposite of the world they'd left behind. Noah was staring straight ahead, out the windshield, with his hands on the steering wheel at exactly ten and two.

"I'm really sorry about your gun." She winced. "I still can't believe I did that. And that I didn't tell you."

"It's okay," Noah said. "You're dealing with something. Consider it over."

Yeah, okay, but that she was dealing with something didn't change the fact that she wished she'd handled it differently. Worry creased the rugged lines of Noah's face. She wondered if it was about her, the auction or the story about his family. She imagined it was all the above.

"What happened to Anne and Caleb?" she asked. "Are they still together?"

He hesitated. She watched as his lips parted, hung open a moment and then closed again. Maybe he'd just been using the fact that she was there as an excuse to talk to himself.

"Long story," he said eventually, without answering her question at all. "How's your head?"

"It's sore," she admitted. "But it feels a lot better than when I was trying to lean backward out of a truck into flashing lights and sirens. Roller coasters are going to be a breeze after this."

"Well, you'll see Anne soon enough," he said, "and she'll be able to give us a better idea of what's going on with your head."

Holly nodded, so did he, and for a long moment she watched as snow-covered fields and trees streamed past them.

"You should've told me," he repeated eventually. "You really should have."

"I know," she said.

Of course, if she'd known how bad it was going to be, she would have. She was a soldier, and yeah, she was stubborn, but she wasn't an idiot. In fact, she had tried to tell him earlier, in the loft, when she'd started admitting she couldn't remember the Imposters' faces—right before he'd made her feel like he wasn't taking her seriously, and she'd accused him of coddling her. And then any thought of telling him about her injury had gone right out the window—and so had she, literally—in some strong-willed drive to show him she was strong. And why? Because she was trying to prove to herself she didn't have a concussion? Because the fact that she'd fit so comfortably into his arms made her feel vulnerable and strange?

"I think falling in love makes people do stupid and foolish things," she said, "and I've never believed in love at first sight. My parents fell head over heels for each other when they met, and were engaged within days. Now they're separated. They split up within days of my entering basic training."

Noah turned and gaped at her. "Where did that come from?"

She wasn't quite sure. Maybe the concussion was impacting her inner filter. Or the fact that Seth had applied for a fake wedding license in her name had reminded her of them.

"You were talking about Caleb and Anne," she said. "You told me they'd fallen in love as teenagers, had two kids together, but from the way you were talking it sounds like they're not together now. Reminded me of my parents. They're technically not divorced, but not together, either."

"Huh," he said. Again, it wasn't an answer. A smattering of buildings came into view. There were small independent stores, a mill of some sort and scattered farms, with fields in between. "I don't know if Caleb and Anne still consider themselves together. I'm guessing she does and he doesn't, but I don't really know. They got married when Drew was a baby. Her parents disowned her, but she had some money her grandparents had left her in savings bonds and was able to use the money to keep them afloat while she went through university. They moved to Ontario and she became a doctor. Drew is almost eighteen now and Lizzy is four. Caleb is currently a long-haul truck driver and away for weeks and months at a time. I don't think you'll meet him."

And while she suspected that was all Noah was going to say for now, something in his tone made her think of the way the sky rumbles before a storm.

His phone buzzed with a text. Noah glanced at the screen and let out a sigh so pained it was like she could feel it move through her.

"That was Liam," he said. "The Brampton safe house has been compromised. He and Seth are now on the run."

SEVEN

On the run? But if they couldn't go to the safe house, where could they go?

"How was it compromised?" she asked. "And where are we going to meet up with everyone now?"

"I don't know," Noah said. He shook his head. "They're scrambling to find somewhere else. He sent me a quick text. Hopefully, he'll be able to get someplace safe and call me back soon."

"But how did the Imposters know where Liam and Seth were heading?" she pressed.

Noah shrugged. "It's possible Snitch5751 supplied them with locations of Toronto-area safe houses. Or it was in the information they stole from Elias's devices."

Suspicion brushed her spine. "Or somebody told them. How much do you trust Mack, Jess and Liam? Is it possible one of them is Snitch5751? Or compromised?"

Something flickered in Noah's eyes, a hesitation, like there was something he still hadn't told her. Then the look hardened to resolve. "No, I know them and trust them with my life. Someone in law enforcement may have helped the Imposters, but not one of them. Not Seth, either."

But how could he be so sure? Questions rattled in her mind, even as Noah started to slow the vehicle to turn and put on his indicator light. She looked up at the farmhouse. It sat alone, high up on a small hill, with what looked like excellent lines of sight in all directions. The house was three stories high, with peeling white paint and a green roof that seemed to be missing a few shingles. A trio of snowmen in mismatched scarves and hats, with crooked pebble smiles, greeted them with outstretched stick arms.

Noah parked the truck, then walked around and opened her door. He didn't offer her his arm, not explicitly, but as she slid from the truck and her boots hit the snow, she found herself reaching for it. He let her take it and she felt the strength of his muscles under her hand. He reached past her and closed the truck door.

"Okay," he said. "Let's do this."

They walked together across the snowy ground. The front door opened before they reached the porch. A woman stood on the doorstep, tall and willowy, in blue jeans and a voluminous white sweater with the sleeves pushed up past her elbows. Her pale blond hair was tied back in a bun. And if Holly hadn't heard her story, and so knew she was in her mid- to late-thirties, she would've imagined her to be a lot younger.

Anne's hands snapped to her hips as her gaze ran over Noah, with a look that seemed very sisterly, and a concerned one at that. Then her attention flittered to Holly's grasp on Noah's arm.

"I'm Anne. You must be Holly." She gestured in welcome. "Come on in."

"Thank you." Holly detangled herself from Noah's arm and followed her into the house. A large living room lay to her left, filled with a huge, real Christmas tree bedecked with homemade ornaments. Ahead of her, a wide wooden staircase led up to the second floor. She caught a glimpse of a young man at the top who she guessed was Drew. He was as willowy and thin as his mother, with a mop of jet-black hair. A small girl with blond curls peeked out from around his knees, likely Lizzy. Noah waved. The little girl waved back. The youth bent and whispered something in her ear, then took her by the hand and gently led her out of sight.

"I've asked them to give us some privacy while I got Holly settled," Anne told Noah, "and promised them their Uncle Nah would be up to say hi as soon as I made sure his friend was okay." Then she turned to Holly. "You can lie down in the den for now. I'll join you in a sec. I just want to talk to Noah for a moment."

She gestured to a door to her right, and Holly glanced through. Tall shelves of obviously well-read books lined the walls. A brightly colored quilt draped across the battered leather couch.

"You need a hand?" Noah asked.

"No, it's okay. I've got it." Holly shrugged her coat off into Noah's waiting hands. But as she leaned down to untie her boots, she felt her head begin to swim.

"Everything okay?" he asked, when she straightened again.

"Actually, bending down like that was making me dizzy…"

"Here, let me." He sank to one knee and untied the laces of her boots. She looked down at him. His hair was wet and tousled from the snow. His face was flushed. And as his gray eyes glanced up at her face, an inescapable thought made her heart skip a beat.

She was attracted to him. Very much so, judging by the odd fluttering in her chest.

No, it had to be the combination of adrenaline and the knock to her head. She'd never been one to have crushes on guys, and this was the worst possible time and place for such a thing. The idea of starting up a romantic relationship with Noah was laughable. It was inappropriate for starters, considering he was a witness protection officer and she was a witness. It could be weeks before she'd be out of witness protection and then, as soon as testifying at the inquiry was done, she'd be deploying back overseas. There was no way she'd give up her career to stay in Canada and be with a man. And no way she'd ever ask him to give up his career to follow her.

And yet, from the strength of character shown in how he'd dealt with everything today, to the curve of his mouth as he smiled, there was something about him that everything inside her was ridiculously drawn to. And when his fingertips brushed her calves as he helped her out of her boots, there was no denying the shiver that ran across her skin.

Help me, Lord. I'm losing my mind.

"Thank you," she said, without meeting his eye.

She walked into the study, feeling Noah's gaze follow her like a sunbeam on her back. She let the door swing shut, lay down on the couch and pulled the blanket over her. She closed her eyes.

"What were you thinking, driving around like that with her in the vehicle?" Anne's voice filtered through the door. "You let her overexert herself and potentially make her concussion worse, when she should've been resting?"

"I didn't let her do anything!" Noah said. "I couldn't stop that woman from 'exerting herself' if I tried!"

"You should have—"

"She climbed out a window onto a ledge three stories off the ground, in a snowstorm!" he retorted, exasperation mixing with something like awe in his voice. For a second his words seemed to hang in the air. Then he laughed, as if he'd suddenly heard what he was saying. "And then, like that wasn't enough, she insisted she could climb up a wall onto a roof without my help. She's…she's impossible."

"Sounds like she's good for you," Anne said. "Someone falls into your life who stubbornly won't let you save her?"

"I don't see how that's good for me!" Noah's voice rose.

Then their voices dropped again, just low enough that she could hear them talking, but couldn't make any words out clearly.

Who did Noah think he was, to call her impossible? He had absolutely no idea who she was, what she'd been through or what she was capable of. And he never would.

"When are we going to talk about Caleb?" Anne's

voice floated back in range. "I have a potential buyer for the gym."

"And I've told you I'm not going to sell it." Noah's voice was back, too. "We'll figure something else out. I promise. Just not that." Rock-and-roll music played. Noah's phone was ringing. "One second, I have to check in with my team. Then as soon as they confirm the details, we'll get back on the road."

"You're not taking her anywhere!" Anne's voice rose.

"With all due respect, you don't understand—" Noah started.

"I'm a doctor, and she's my patient," Anne cut him off. "So make yourself comfortable."

"I'm telling you right now, she won't agree to rest," Noah said.

Anne didn't even answer. Instead, she pushed through the door into the study. Holly sat up.

"How are you feeling?" Anne asked.

"Impossible, apparently," she answered. "And don't worry, I'm not about to run off into some hail of bullets just to spite him."

"But you're tempted to?" Something twinkled in Anne's eyes.

"Just a little," Holly admitted.

Anne chuckled, then grabbed a chair, pulled it over and sat. "Noah is the most stubborn man I know. Especially when he's trying to solve everyone else's problems instead of focusing on his own. But his heart is always in the right place. Now, let's check you out."

She ran smoothly and professionally through a series of tests, from checking Holly's eyes to some simple coordination and word games. Even before she gave her verdict Holly could tell she was sluggish. It was like she'd been running on adrenaline and fear, and now that it was done she could feel her body wanting to shut down. Resignation swept over her, reminding her of the looks she'd seen in injured soldiers the moment they gave up fighting to survive, and realized it was time to switch to the hard work of getting better. "Let me guess. I've got a concussion."

"Certainly looks that way," Anne said.

Holly lay back against the pillow. *Well, God, now what?*

"Thankfully, it seems to be pretty minor," Anne stated. "Your pupils are the same size and you've got no major lag in response time. Your verbal response time is slow, but your language skills are still coherent. You just need rest. I'm going to suggest you spend three days here, resting completely for the first twenty-four hours, and then if you're up to it you can move to a new safe house."

"But you have kids!" Holly sat up. "I'm a witness in a federal parliamentary inquiry. Plus, I have criminals after me."

"It's okay." Anne gently pushed her back against the couch. "This isn't my first rodeo." There was an edge to her voice, strong like tempered steel, that reminded Holly of what Noah had said about Anne's childhood. "I'm not in the habit of throwing people who need help to the wolves. Noah will sit up and keep guard at night. And while this house may be old, it has a state-of-the-art security system, reinforced locks on all the doors and windows, and a passage from the cold cellar that leads to the barn out back. Lizzy will sleep in my room and go to work with me during the day. She won't leave my sight. Drew is almost eighteen and better in a crisis than most adults I know. Plus, he's a crack shot with a gun, as am I, if it comes to that. But it won't. Because nothing Noah's told me about the people after you leads us to think they're about to storm a farmhouse."

"True," Holly admitted. "But they might set fire to Drew's school or your practice and show up dressed as firefighters."

"Okay," Anne said. "When you know your enemy, you can prepare against that."

That was very true. Again, Holly wondered what kind of enemies Anne had faced in her life. Considering the type of cyber terrorists the Imposters were, and with the amount of time and energy it would take to process the data they'd stolen from Elias and prepare it for the online auction on Christmas Eve, it was more likely they'd wait and watch, like trappers, for Holly to reemerge.

"Okay," she said, "but at the first sign of trouble, we're going to leave. No argument."

"Or I'll take the kids and go," Anne said. "Either way, we'll wait and see. I'll watch you carefully over the next couple of days for signs of any major complications. If something worsens, I'm going to insist on taking you to the hospital. But for now, I'm prescribing twenty-four hours of strict bed rest, followed by another forty-eight of easing you back into normal life."

Right. It felt like the entire world was on fire. Prosecutors had to be questioning where their star witness had gone. RCMP had to have started letting hundreds of witnesses know their new identities were about to be auctioned off, giving them days to pack up and run. And here Holly was going to be lying around in the dark, not helping, not fighting and doing absolutely nothing. She was vaguely aware of Anne saying something comforting and leaving the room. But the frustration that burned inside her was so strong she could barely hear her.

What's happening to my life, Lord? I did everything right. I served my country honorably. I stepped up to testify against General Bertie. Why is this happening to me?

She lay back on the couch, feeling her hands ball into fists. There was a soft rap on the door. She looked up as Noah leaned through the doorway. "Can I come in?"

"Sure." She shifted to make room for him. "I'm really sorry about all this."

"I know," he said. "And you can stop apologizing at any time. I mean, it's no fun for me to stay annoyed at someone who's this miserable."

Despite herself, a laugh slipped from her lips. He sat down beside her on the couch. It sagged as his weight shifted the pillow, and she found her shoulder bumping against his.

"I'm sorry," she said again.

"It's fine." He raised his arm and stretched it across the top of the couch, making more room for her. "I don't mind if you lean against me. Just stretch in whatever way you need to be comfortable. Believe me, I've been crammed into smaller spaces with Liam and Mack than this."

Yeah, but this man had no idea she was attracted to him.

"Either that or I sit on the floor," Noah offered.

"No, it's cool, thank you," she said quickly. She shifted her position again and felt the strength of his forearm against her shoulder. It was strong, solid and soft all at once. The smell of him filled her senses. It was a warm and outdoorsy smell, like cocoa at night by a bonfire.

"I'm sure you've fought way harder battles than this before," he said.

"Than lying around in the dark doing nothing?"

"Than overcoming and fighting your own instincts," he said. "Believe me, I know that sometimes the hardest thing is doing nothing."

She wanted to ask him what he'd meant by that. Instead she said, "Status update?"

"Lizzy said you're pretty and asked me if I'm going to marry you," Noah said. She felt a flush rushing to her cheeks. "Also, nobody made it to the safe house."

He shifted and somehow his arm seemed to move even closer. It was way more distracting than it had any right to be. "When Liam and Seth got there, three police cars were parked outside and cops were searching the place. Apparently someone reported it as a drug operation."

"How did they know which safe house you'd be trying to take me to?"

"They didn't," Noah said. "Apparently various threats were called in at various locations to local police in the area. Anywhere within an hour's drive of Toronto. We're talking fires, break-ins, children in danger, medical emergencies—dozens of false alarms. Authorities across the province are scrambling, trying to figure out who's placing so many nuisance calls. It's the biggest single waste of law enforcement time in provincial history."

"It's smart," Holly said, "using law enforcement to try and flush us out. And since there's no way to know where the Imposters are, it keeps me from going to get help."

"It gets better, or worse, depending on your perspective," Noah said. "Jess had the bright idea of checking herself into the hospital, considering she's already wearing your jacket, and so anyone following her might think she's you. Mack took her to an emergency room in Mississauga, still in that wig Seth gave her, and checked her in under 'Hildy Ashes.' Within ten minutes a nurse came over and offered to take her to a private room. According to Seth, our hacker friend the Wraith had planted an emergency alert in the computer system of every hospital in southern Ontario reporting that someone with a name similar to yours has a very contagious disease and would need to be quarantined. Needless to say they got out of there."

"Wow," Holly said.

"You sound almost impressed."

"I just appreciate the Imposters' tactics," she said. "There are only two of them. Two! One that's the tech genius and one that's the heavy. It's incredibly difficult for two people to take on something huge, especially while staying hidden, and hiring mercenaries to do your dirty work for you is risky." She thought back to the three criminals someone had hired to threaten her out of testifying against General Bertie, subsequently driving her into witness protection. "So, they resort to guerrilla tactics and urban terrorism. Police aren't equipped to handle it."

"Well, it's pushing us to accelerate our countertactics and proceed without debriefing," Noah said. "Liam's taking Seth to a new location now. Not a witness protection safe house, mind you, but somewhere only Seth knows. Then he's going to start pulling on threads within the police to see what he can find. Jess is preparing to go back into work tomorrow morning, and Mack's already gone underground to see what he can sniff out through criminal sources."

Yeah, she'd heard all that back at the loft, but now that her head felt clearer it made even less sense. "But what about the cases they're assigned to? What about their regular work?" She blinked as something Elias had said suddenly twigged at the back of her brain. "Hang on, I think before he died Elias said you weren't even cleared to work."

Was that true? It couldn't be! How could she possibly forget something like that, even temporarily? Yet, as she watched, Noah sighed and pulled his arm away.

"There's something I need to tell you," he murmured. "Something I should've told you a few hours ago."

No. She shook her head. No, he wouldn't have kept anything important like that from her. She'd trusted him. She'd let him bring her here.

"Elias was right," she said. "You are on leave. I apologized to you, like, six times for not telling you about the concussion, and you kept that from me?"

"I'm not on leave—" Noah started.

She cut him off. "Then what did he mean—"

"It's complicated—"

"Not good enough!" She heard her voice rise. "You asked me to trust you with my life."

"I was offered a really big promotion a week ago," Noah said. "A desk job in Ottawa coordinating a team of officers and protecting very high level federal witnesses. But it required a higher level of security clearance than I currently have. And I don't want to apply for that right now because it means the feds go poking around, doing a deep dive into your life, looking for any potential vulnerabilities. So my boss suggested I use up the month of holiday time I've been banking to think it through."

She blinked. "So, you're on vacation?"

"Yup." A wry smile battled the frustration in his eyes. "This is how I'm spending my Christmas vacation. Everyone I pulled together to help me is off active duty for one reason or another. Liam was beaten into a coma last summer when his cover was blown and he's still on medical leave until March. Mack was suspended for six months for some personal reason he hasn't told me the details of. And Jess was given the choice of a six-week suspension or human resources training following something that happened to her in the past. She'd taken the suspension, but now she's going back in tomorrow and biting the bullet, in order to be our ears and eyes on the inside. I'm sorry I didn't tell you all this earlier, but I didn't know how you'd react, and things have kind of been crazy ever since you and I met."

Yeah, she could agree with that. She sat back on the couch and looked at him for a long moment. "So, you assembled a team of rogue RCMP agents to take down a pair of urban terrorists, root out a snitch in law enforcement and stop criminals from buying hundreds of witness protection identities."

"I did." He crossed his arms and something fierce flashed like fire in his eyes. "I also have a former criminal hacker on my team. And hopefully, a military corporal who, unless she turns herself in at an RCMP station fairly soon, people are going to assume is either dead or has walked away from witness protection."

Now he told her. She eyed him thoughtfully.

He was every bit as stubborn, strong-willed and crazy as she was.

"So you're saying that if I don't report in to RCMP witness protection and get assigned to a new officer, they're just going to think I ditched police protection?" she clarified.

"Yeah," he said. "Happens all the time. People just disappear from the witness protection system. Thanks to Seth's fake trail of bread crumbs, they'll think you ran off to elope with a Mr. Smith, rent an apartment in Vancouver and travel to England."

Was he trying to be funny?

"You should've told me all this before," she said.

His chin rose. "I know."

Then she reached for his hand. His arms unfolded and he enveloped her palm in his.

"I'm in," she said. "Just don't ever sideline me or keep anything from me ever again."

"Deal." He shook her hand, then released it. "And there's one more major piece of the puzzle Seth's looking into. He thinks Snitch5751 is also the person who hired those three criminals who attacked you and drove you into witness protection."

* * *

He watched as her eyes widened. Fear washed over her features and both her hands began to shake. He reached out, but she didn't let him take them. "You're saying those three men who attacked me were hired by the same guy who gave the Imposters the information they needed to kill Elias and steal the witness protection files?"

"That's Seth's working theory," Noah said. "He might not be right."

"Every single life that's being threatened by this auction has been because of me!" Her voice rose. "Every vulnerable witness whose secret identity is now on the chopping block to the highest bidder is because I agreed to testify against General Bertie about some missing weapons on the other side of the world."

She was shaking so hard now she was shivering. And Noah wanted more than anything to wrap his arms around her and tell her no, it wasn't possible, no, it couldn't be true.

"Maybe!" he said. "I don't know. It's what Seth thinks happened."

He stretched his hands out, palms up, willing her to take them. She slowly complied, sliding her hands into his. He wrapped his fingers around hers, and they held each other like survivors ready to pull one another up a cliff.

"Maybe Snitch5751 is more than one person," he suggested. "Maybe he hoped those men would kill you, and when that didn't work he used the Imposters to come after you in exchange for the files. Maybe a different criminal found the first criminal's signal and used it to mask their identity. We can't know." He pulled her in closer, wishing he could hold her against his chest and wrap his arms around her. "But we'll find out. We'll stop that auction, we'll save the witnesses and you'll testify before the inquiry about Bertie's crimes. I promise."

"Okay." And as her green eyes looked into his, he could tell she believed him. He just prayed he wouldn't let her down.

Anne knocked on the door just then to let them know Lizzy's room was ready if Holly wanted to lie down.

And Noah found himself spending the next three days playing with Lizzy, looking over Drew's film school portfolio's sketches and designs for special effect movie makeup and creature design, maneuvering his way around the difficult conversations Anne still wanted to have about Caleb, coordinating with his team remotely whenever possible and waiting as Holly rested and healed.

The work and family parts of the equation were fairly simple. Despite their best efforts, Liam and Mack seemed to be hitting nothing but false leads and dead ends. Jess reported that while the RCMP had their best officers on it, none seemed closer to finding the Imposters, and were focusing their energies on warning witnesses as they scrambled to find them new homes and identities on short notice. Seth confirmed that while the Imposters were lying low in the real world, they were busy online promoting their evil and despicable upcoming auction to every lowlife in the dark web world.

But if that side of Noah's life was filled with frustration and darkness, spending time at the country house with the family was filled with all the excitement and joy of the impending holidays. He helped Lizzy bake cookies and Drew put up Christmas lights around the house. They built more snowmen and a series of tunnels and forts. Between Lizzy's enthusiasm and innocence, and Drew's quiet and intense creativity, Noah quickly realized just how deeply he'd missed them both.

No, it was that last part of the equation he found one of the biggest challenges—watching over Holly as she healed. Being there, day in and day out, seeing the frustration burning in her face as she painstakingly followed Anne's instructions to do nothing for as much of the day as possible. He found himself pacing while she slept, waiting for her to reappear at the door. It was like something inside him kept tugging his heart, mind and attention toward her and he didn't know why. He sat with her in the den, with the lights low, telling her stories about his cases, his childhood, what it had been like to grow up in a fostering family and the various foster siblings that had come through his life. He told her stories that made her laugh and stories that he'd never told anybody, because she told him listening to his voice helped her relax.

He enjoyed sitting beside her at the family dinner table, watching as she slowly drew his nephew out in conversation, enjoyed listening as she played dolls with Lizzy. On the second day, she sat with Drew for hours as Noah's shy nephew showed her the drawings and designs in his film school portfolio, of monsters and fantastical creatures, and then sketched both the Ghoul and the Wraith as she described them the best she could from memory. Noah sent the sketches to Seth, who ran them through the database, but got no hits. Liam, Mack and

Jess sent them dozens of pictures of potential suspects—
both law enforcement and criminal mug shots—none
of which Holly recognized, either. Then, when Anne
signed off on it, Noah and Holly started going for short
walks in the snow around the farmhouse, bundled up
with hoods over their heads, shoulders occasionally
bumping, as Holly got back her full health.

He liked her company more than he'd ever liked anybody else's. He liked how she listened to people. He respected her inner fight and drive, and how she never
complained.

Corporal Hildegard "Holly" Asher was an impres-
sive, interesting, determined and tough-as-anything
person—and he knew he had no right being attracted
to her the way he was. She was vulnerable and in his
protection. Showing any interest would be an abuse
of power, ungentlemanly and wrong. It wasn't like
she could easily walk away if she didn't feel the same
way about him. Plus, if her story about her parents had
taught her anything, it was not to believe in whirlwind
romances. If he told her how he felt now, it would put
her in an unforgivably awkward and uncomfortable
position. He would not, could not, do that to her. Sure,
maybe some real and lasting romances started in situ-
ations as awkward as theirs. But not for him and not
with a woman like Holly.

These were the thoughts that tumbled through his
mind as he walked slowly around the house three days
after the attack. The sun glittered off the fields of endless white, so bright it almost hurt his eyes. Holly
walked beside him, shrouded in a large coat she'd borrowed from Anne, the hood with a fake fur trim that

hid her face, so that only her nose and keen eyes shone through.

"Any news from the team?" she asked, as they strolled slowly side by side.

She was no doubt thrilled to be able to get out of the house and walk, even though he could tell that she wanted to break into a sprint.

"Nothing concrete," he said. "We've looked over all the pictures they've sent. Law enforcement is stretched to the max trying to relocate witnesses, but it's like trying to evacuate a sinking ship while simultaneously building new lifeboats. Even if we did relocate everyone, none of their new lives are going to be as secure as the stolen ones. And the amount of information in each witness file going up on the auction block would still give criminals complete data on everything we know about each one, and a great head start in finding them again. The bigger problem is some witnesses feel so upset, angry and betrayed about authorities letting this happen that they'd rather take their lives and safety into their own hands." He paused and looked at her. "How's the headache?"

"Almost nonexistent when I'm lying still and moving slowly," Holly said. "But it shows up like a swift kick when I move my head too quickly. How's Seth doing?"

Noah liked the way she asked questions. They were sharp, direct and pointed, even when she had an aching head and was moving slowly. There was something about having her around that made him a better cop.

"Frustrated," he answered. "He's watching online as the auction ticks closer and closer and isn't able to stop it."

Holly sighed. Noah imagined she knew the feeling.

"When does the auction go live?" she asked.

"Noon on Christmas Eve."

"We're going to find them," she stated. "I don't know how, but we're going to find Snitch5751, catch the Imposters and stop the auction before anyone gets hurt. I have faith."

Noah smiled and looked up to the cloudless sky above. *Do I have faith, God?* It had been more than seventy-two hours since Elias had been killed, and they still didn't have a solid lead.

"What are you going do once this is all over?" he asked.

She stopped walking and turned toward him. "You mean when I'm fully healed from the concussion, the auction has been halted, Snitch5751 and the Imposters are all behind bars and I've testified against General Bertie at the inquiry?"

"Yes." He chuckled. "After all of that."

"I'm going to redeploy," she said. "I'm heading back into whatever war zone the military sends me. I knew from a really young age that I was put on this earth to serve others. It's my calling and my passion."

They were standing so close that a braver or more foolish man might've tried to reach out and take her hand. An even bolder and more foolish one might've even asked if he could kiss her.

"Do you regret going into witness protection?" he asked.

The question seemed to spread out into the wintry air between them. Wisps of dark hair brushed her face as she looked into his eyes. And he knew without a doubt she was the most interesting person he'd ever met.

"No," she said softly. "I don't. Because as much as I resented having to do it at first, I know I did it for the right reasons. I had a responsibility to stay alive to testify. And…"

"And?" he asked quietly.

"And while I wish with every fiber of my being that I didn't have a concussion, hadn't missed the shot at the Ghoul and could remember the Imposters' faces, I don't regret being here, in this, with you."

"I'm glad you're here, too," he said.

His hands bumped against hers. Then slowly, cautiously, he felt their fingers begin to link.

His phone began to ring just then. Noah stepped back, pulled his hands away and reached for it, heat rising to his face as if somehow the person on the other end of the line could read his mind and tell what he was thinking. He glanced at the screen.

"Hi, Seth."

"Hey, how's my favorite detective doing?" the hacker asked.

"Not bad," Noah said. "What's up? Everything okay?"

"Yeah," Seth said. "How soon can you be here? The false leads I've created for Holly are getting a lot of attention and I haven't found the Imposters yet, but I think I might've found out exactly where Snitch5751 was when he messaged the Imposters."

EIGHT

Holly watched as Noah stepped back and took the call. She could feel her heart pounding in her chest. Had that really happened? Had she just come close to blurting out to Noah that she was attracted to him? Had she really stood there in the snow, holding his hand like they were teenagers, when there were so many more important things going on? She turned and walked a few paces, gazing toward the wintry horizon and hoping Noah would think she was just giving him privacy for his phone call.

Help me, Lord. I don't understand my heart or my mind now. All I know is they're tugging me toward this man I've just met and am only starting to get to know.

She turned back and looked at his strong, handsome form silhouetted against the sky.

He ran his gloved hand over the strong lines of his jaw. "Okay, I'll see you there." Noah clicked off the phone and turned back. "So, as you likely heard, that was Seth. Long story short, he thinks he might've figured out where Snitch5751 sent his messages to the Imposters from. But it's raw data and he's still processing it. He's hoping by the time I get there he'll have something more concrete for me."

Relief flooded his face. He glanced to the sky and she watched as the words *Thank You, God* moved across his lips. Then he turned back to her. "I think we've got a lead, and I'm going to go check it out."

"*We're* going to check it out," she said.

He'd already taken two steps toward the house when the sound of her voice made him stop. "No, I'm going. You're staying here. You were in an accident and you're still recovering from a concussion."

"Yes, and I've been recovering." She crossed her arms. "Anne said I was okay to go on short drives."

"Around town!" His hands flew up in the air. "To get coffee! Not to go see someone in witness protection about locating a pair of cyber terrorists!"

"Who is sitting in front of a computer in a safe house!" She mimicked his gesture, as if they were both fighting an invisible enemy that had suddenly materialized between them. "Please, Noah, I've been stuck doing nothing for seventy-two hours. I'm the only one of us who's seen the Imposters, so I'm the only one who will recognize them if they run into you."

Noah's head was shaking. She knew what he was about to say.

Couldn't he see how much she needed to get out of the house and do something, even if it was just sitting in a truck for half an hour and listening to whatever intel Seth had dug up?

"What if the Imposters spot you and try to kidnap or kill you?" he argued.

"Then you'll be there to have my back!" she said. "You think I'm going to be safer here without you?"

She watched as his jaw clenched and his eyes rose to the sky. The long pause that followed was punctuated only by the whistling wind and her own chattering teeth.

"Yes!" Noah said finally. "I think you'll be safer here alone then coming to see Seth with me. Because I think the Imposters don't know you're here. I think they're much more likely to find you if we go out in the world. So I think you're wrong. Totally wrong."

Was she? She'd thought she'd been pretty convincing, actually.

"What do I have to say to convince you?" she asked.

"I don't think you can!" Noah said. Then as she watched, his shoulders fell. "But I also recognize that you're a soldier. You're clearly plenty tough and strong enough to handle yourself. You've got a better sense of how your head is feeling than I do, and you're not a prisoner here. As you know, the fact that you didn't report into witness protection and get assigned a new officer after Elias died means technically you're not even in witness protection anymore! So I don't actually have any right to tell you what to do."

Wow. She rocked back on her heels.

For a long moment he didn't say anything. Neither did she. What could she say? She'd been gearing up for a fight and he'd just dropped his hands and stepped out of the ring.

"Thank you," she said at last, not knowing what else to say. "Trust me, I'm not about to do something stupid or risky."

"I believe you." He crossed his arms. "Even though you climbed out a window."

"Three days ago!" She cut him off. "Before I realized I had a concussion, and then saw a doctor and took three days' prescribed rest!"

"I'm not fighting you on this," Noah said. "Just because I don't think you're right doesn't mean I don't think your points are valid. I actually agree that leaving you isn't ideal, either." He blew out a long breath. "Okay, here's what I want to do. I want to ask Anne if she's okay with it. If not, we'll find another solution. I'd also like you to take it slow and not push yourself past the breaking point. If anything dangerous or even suspicious goes down I'm turning around and bringing you back here, okay?"

She nodded. Yeah, all that was fair. And he was actually being nicer about it than she probably would've been if the tables were turned.

"Also, you're going to need a disguise. Not a makeshift Seth disguise. An actual good one."

"Deal." For a moment she was even tempted to reach out and shake his hand.

"Good," he said. "Because I would really hate it if something bad happened to you."

"I'd hate it if something bad happened to you, too."

A flicker of that smile she was really growing to like turned up the corners of his lips again.

"Right. Then we first go talk to Anne. After that we'll see what we can do to make you look less like yourself."

They started back toward the house.

Noah seemed resigned when Anne cleared Holly

to go, with pretty much the same restrictions he had placed—like paying attention to her symptoms, taking it slow and resting if the headache came back. Then Noah led Holly upstairs and knocked on Drew's door. The young man opened it and Holly realized it didn't actually lead to a bedroom, but a stairwell leading up to an attic room above. Drew's eyebrows rose in an expression that reminded her of his uncle.

"Holly needs a disguise," Noah said. "Something simple that makes her not look like herself. I was wondering if you had something she could borrow."

Drew's lips turned up quizzically and a smile crinkled the corners of his eyes. "All right, come on."

They followed him up the stairs and came out in a long space with slanting walls. She gasped. It was a workshop. Elaborate masks of alien creatures and animals smiled, snarled and stared at her. Jars and tubes of paint and an array of brushes spilled across a large table.

Holly pressed her hand to her lips. She knew Drew wanted to get into movie special effects makeup and had seen the pictures in his portfolio. But she'd never imagined he was capable of anything like this.

For a long moment Drew just stood there with his arms crossed, somehow managing to look both a lot older and younger than seventeen at the same time. Then he turned to his uncle. "Give us twenty minutes?"

Noah nodded. "Sounds good. I have some phone calls to make. Don't make her look like a goblin or an elf." He glanced at Holly. "Meet you downstairs."

When he'd left, she frowned at Drew. "Tell me he's not going to leave without me," she said.

"He wouldn't." The youth shook his head. "Uncle Nah is a really good guy."

He pulled a stool over to the table and waved her toward it. She sat.

"Why do you call him Uncle Nah?" she asked.

"It's my dad's nickname for him." Drew shrugged. "No-Nah. I think it goes back to when they were teenagers, because he tried to stop him from doing anything fun." His shoulders rose and fell, like he wasn't committing to either side of the argument.

Caleb. Even after all the time she'd spent in the house she didn't know much about him, including why he wasn't home with his family for Christmas.

"I think you're better off with extensions than a wig," Drew said. "Wigs fall off, and extensions can last for days. It's what movies use for more serious stunt work."

"Sounds good." She'd never had long hair and never wanted it. And it wasn't like Noah was about to be okay with her doing anything that would remotely qualify as a stunt. Still, anything was better than another wig.

"All I've got is special effects movie makeup," he said. "It's a lot thicker than regular makeup, but applied the right way it can be even more effective than a fake nose or plastic appliance. Again, those tear and fall off, too. My mom will no doubt have clothes you can borrow. And I have some contacts that will change the color of your eyes."

So she really was going to look nothing like herself.

She watched as he busied himself setting up the hair extensions.

"Your work is incredible," she said.

"Thank you." Again, she noticed that although his lips

were slow to smile, pride hovered behind the guarded shield in his eyes.

"You're Corporal Hildegard Asher, aren't you?" he asked. "I've been following the inquiry into General Bertie online."

Her heart stuttered a beat. "You haven't told anyone, have you?"

"Of course not." Drew rolled his eyes. "The internet says you're somewhere in British Columbia, eloping with some guy named Smith and going to England?"

She snorted. "Don't believe everything you read online."

"Lizzy's apparently telling everyone at church and preschool that you're marrying Uncle Nah," he said. "And Mom just told me you needed help. Is that why you're here? Because people want to hurt you for telling the inquiry Bertie gave weapons to people overseas?"

She nodded. "It's a lot bigger than that now. But yeah, that was the start of it."

He opened another drawer and started pulling out various pots of makeup, heavier and brighter than anything she'd ever worn before.

"I had problems with some kids at school," he said, again not quite looking at her. "Really bad stuff. Everybody knew it was happening, but nobody would admit it." He shuddered as if trying to shake off the memory. "But my mom would notice bruises and stuff, because she's a doctor, right? Then she'd go in and raise a fuss. And finally one kid came out and said yeah, I was being hurt. And it was hard to explain, but it was one of the best moments of my life, right? Because the bullying was out there. It wasn't hidden anymore. And I figure what you're doing is really brave. Because everybody loves General Bertie. People talk about his service record and huge charity Christmas parties like he walks on water. And you're pointing out he made mistakes. And that takes guts."

"Thank you," she murmured, not knowing what else to say. "I'm sorry kids at school were mean to you."

"Thanks." He nodded. "Some people think it's weird for a guy to be this into the arts and creating movie creatures."

"Or a girl to be into the army," Holly said.

This time a genuine smile flashed across his lips and for the first time his eyes really met hers. "Yeah, I guess that, too. Uncle Nah was really supportive. Mom was great, too."

"And your dad?" she asked.

"He doesn't understand me, and he doesn't get me," Drew said. "But he loves me and that's good enough for now. Lizzy told him you and Uncle Nah were getting married on Christmas Eve, and Mom had to set him straight."

The mental image of Noah standing by an altar in a tuxedo with a ring in his hand crossed her mind. She shoved it away. "Well, that's ridiculous. And why Christmas Eve?"

"I think she overheard something my mom and Noah were saying about how Christmas Eve is the big event." He paused and looked up at her. "I'm guessing it's not a good event?"

"No, it's not," she said. "In fact, it's a very bad thing. You and your family are safe. But other people could get very hurt."

"Is there anything I can do to help?" he asked, and her heart ached for this earnest young man and everything he'd already been through.

"You already are."

"Cool." He opened a small box. Six flat vials of colored disks lay inside. "Now, if you don't mind, I'm going to put your contacts in first."

Twenty-five minutes later she was standing back in the front hallway of the farmhouse staring in the mirror at a person she'd never seen before. Smooth and strategic lines of thick movie makeup had made her cheekbones look both sharper and pinker. Another shade of pink made her lips look shiny and fuller. Long cascading locks of dark hair fell around her face and shoulders, all the way to her back. Bright turquoise eyes blinked out at her under dark fake lashes.

She slid her arms through the sleeves of another one of Anne's coats. This one was a bright green and made her think of lime candy, with a hood of fuzzy fake fur.

Come on, Holly. You have a job to do. An outside is just an outside. It has no bearing on who you really are.

The door opened, and she stepped back.

"Holly, you ready to go?" Noah said. "I got new license plates on the truck and the snow brushed off, and— Whoa."

Noah's words caught in his throat. He stood there for a moment and watched as he struggled for words.

"Wow." He ran his hand over the back of his neck. "I thought Drew might lend you a wig or something. But this is… Yeah, sorry. You look really different."

She shoved her feet into her boots. "I know, I look ridiculous."

"No, no, not at all," Noah raised his hands, palms up. "I didn't mean that at all. You look pretty, actually."

Pretty. The word hit her like a punch to the gut. No man in her entire life had ever told her she looked pretty before. Was that all it took? A ton of paint on her face? Fake hair and lashes? But as her eyes searched his face, she saw something there that made it even worse.

Detective Noah Wilder was blushing.

Oh, no. Through all those hugs, walks and long conversations. All those times he'd reached for her hands and her for his... Why hadn't she seen it before?

The man she was attracted to liked her back.

Only he was attracted to a fake version of her, who wasn't who she really was at all.

Well, Noah, of all the dumb things you've ever said in your life, that was definitely the dumbest.

Noah was still mentally kicking himself as they drove silently down snowy Ontario back roads toward the safe house. The look on her face as he'd foolishly blurted out that he thought she was pretty had told him everything he needed to know. She'd looked offended. Worse than that, she'd looked hurt. And every awkward apology he'd attempted since then had only made the awkwardness between them worse, until he'd given up, gotten in the truck with her and started driving.

Pretty? Was that the best he could come up with? She was way beyond pretty. Whatever she was, that word didn't even come close. She was fierce. She was strong. She was dynamic. She was a force to be reckoned with. And she was beautiful, too, in a way that shone through all the ridiculous gunk on her face.

And he couldn't begin to let himself think about her that way.

Houses decked in Christmas decorations streamed past the window. Strings of unlit lights wove around the trees. It seemed everyone had collectively decided a few years ago that huge, inflatable, billowing Christmas figures were the must-have thing, and now most lawns were littered with the flat corpses waiting to be inflated again at night.

Four days until Christmas. Three days until the auction went live.

He prayed Seth's lead would change all that.

"Drew told me about the trouble he had in school," Holly said, after a silence so long and excruciating it had seemed to stretch out forever. "I get the impression it was a lot worse than he was letting on."

Yeah, Noah's heart still twisted in knots when he remembered. "He was bullied pretty badly. He's a tough kid, but no one should go through that."

"I've always wished more kids who had trouble at school, like Drew, or at home, like Anne, were encouraged to join the military cadets," she said. "The army has been such a great family to me. At its best it teaches teamwork, self-esteem, independence, service to others…" Her voice trailed off in a sigh. "Which is why it really hurt to see what it can be at its worst."

Noah nodded. Yeah, he could imagine. "When I applied for that promotion I was considering inviting Drew to live with me during college," he said. "Just to give him one less financial worry."

"That's kind of you," she said.

Was it? Well, it wasn't going to happen without the promotion to Ottawa. Not while he was still crisscross-

ing the county helping vulnerable witnesses, a countless number of which were now on the verge of losing
everything.

"Can we ask Seth to get a message to my parents?"
Holly asked. "I imagine he has some encrypted, untrace-
able way of sending emails. They weren't expecting
to see me this Christmas. They knew I was going into
witness protection. And we never tended to do much to
celebrate the holiday, because it was also my birthday,
and my dad was usually working. But I'd still like to
wish them a Merry Christmas and let them know I'm
safe and thinking of them. Oh, and to ignore any online
rumors Seth planted about my getting married."

"I'm sure he can do that," Noah said. "Where are
they?"

"Right now, my mom's in Vancouver and my dad's
on a base in Germany. But they both said they were
going to come to Ottawa for the inquiry when it's my
turn to testify."

He blinked. "I had no idea your parents were on opposite sides of the world."

"There's a lot you don't know about me," she said.
She settled back in the seat and looked out the window,
and he lost sight of her face behind the ridiculously
fluffy hood and mass of hair. "My dad's always served
in the Canadian military. Like I told you, he met my
mother when he was home on leave. She was running
a small garden center at the time. She's a horticulturalist. It was whirlwind, gut-punch, love at first sight."
Holly sighed, as if thinking about more than she was
saying. "She gave everything up to follow him around
the world and be an army wife."

"And you said it didn't work out?" he asked.

"No, it didn't," she said. "My mom tried very, very hard to be the best possible army wife she could, for years. But the constant moves were draining. She missed working. She missed her garden. She missed putting down roots—metaphorically and literally. When I enlisted she moved out to Vancouver to help friends with their garden center business, and never came back. Now they're separated."

"How many times did you move, growing up?" he asked.

"Nineteen," she said. "But at least I always felt at home in the military. Not everyone has that."

Funny, he'd never thought of her as someone who'd had a rough childhood, but he'd known a few individuals who'd moved that many times or more. In his experience, it made people slow to trust, slow to open up and even slower to believe anything permanent could be possible.

They lapsed back into silence again and he thought about Caleb, and why in all the conversations he and Holly had, he'd never really opened up about his foster brother. He'd caught enough snatches of telephone conversation to know that Lizzy had fully and enthusiastically informed her father that he was there, and he knew Anne had talked to him, too. But Caleb had yet to ask to speak to Noah, and he hadn't asked to talk to him, either. Despite Anne's pleas to let Caleb sell the gym they owned together, Noah hadn't visited the property or agreed to meet the potential buyers. He'd meant to visit the gym, he really had, not to sell it as Anne wanted, but to see what state his brother had left it in.

Bros Gym was a painful monument to Noah's attempt to do right by Caleb, and how very badly that had gone wrong.

Caleb had always been the kind of man who needed a little help to keep his life on track, and the gym was supposed to give him that. Time and time again, Caleb had squandered or gambled away whatever money he'd earned, borrowed or won in self-destructive ways, racking up debts and draining his bank account no sooner than money had come in. When Noah's parents had decided to leave Caleb an inheritance, it had been in the hopes he'd use it to make something of himself. They'd hoped owning his own business would give him accountability, stability, purpose and a goal.

At least that had been the plan.

Noah would become the silent partner in the venture and Caleb would be able to use the money Noah's parents had left him to fulfill his dreams, run a business he loved and support his family. Noah had taken his life savings, plus the money he himself had inherited from his parents, and invested it in helping Caleb, Anne, Drew and Lizzy have the best possible shot at life. It's what Noah's parents would've wanted.

In exchange, Caleb would keep on top of the mortgage and all the bills. He'd go back to rehab for his gambling addiction and take college business courses. He'd make good on Noah's investment in him.

Only he hadn't. Three years on and the gym lay empty and abandoned, with utilities cut off from lack of payment, a mortgage in arrears and creditors sending notices to Noah demanding their money.

If it wasn't for the painful knowledge of how Caleb

would blow his share of the money once the building sold, robbing his family of the one major asset they had, Noah would've divested himself of it in a heartbeat. The gym and his relationship to Caleb were now a liability he'd have to disclose in order to get the higher level security clearance a promotion would require. That could lead to investigators poking into Caleb's life to see what kind of man Noah was in business with, and to determine if the gym left Noah vulnerable to either criminal activity or bribery. Now Anne wanted Noah to give up, sell the property and let both himself and Caleb have the share of money they'd invested into it back. And how was that responsible? To give up on his foster brother's best lifeline to turn his circumstances around, and instead give him a lump sum of cash to gamble and party away?

Maybe Anne had given up on Caleb ever changing his mind, coming back, reopening the gym and becoming a better man, but Noah hadn't.

Noah pulled off the rural highway and onto a smaller road, following the GPS directions Seth had given him. A series of dilapidated structures came into view, scattered along the roadside like the remnants of some toy building set that someone had forgotten to tidy up. Then he saw the hangar, old and abandoned, with the carcasses of long-neglected motorboats scattered around the yard. The parking lot lay cold and empty. He didn't much like knowing that Seth had been staying out here all alone for the past few days, without anyone babysitting him. But witness protection was about setting someone up in a safe and secret life, not about providing around-the-clock security. And Seth had never been one for being babysat.

Noah pulled in and dialed Seth's number. It rang. There was no answer.

"You think something's wrong?" Holly asked.

"Hopefully not." He turned off the truck and got out, with Mack's gun in the holster by his side and Holly one step behind him. He watched as her hand twitched toward him, and he realized she probably missed carrying a weapon. But could she shoot one? "Now, stay behind me, and keep a lookout, okay?"

She nodded. He led the way across the parking lot to a plain metal door in the wall. It swung open easily when he grasped the handle, and they stepped into a wood-paneled room that he guessed had once been an office. The place was stifling, as if a dozen space heaters had been turned on full blast. He coughed and raised a hand to his face.

"Seth!" he called. "Hey, are you here?"

No answer.

The room had been both trashed and tossed. Broken monitors, smashed computers and shards of glass covered the floor. The smell of gasoline hung heavy in the air. He stepped farther into the room and she followed, their feet crunching on broken glass. Then he saw Seth's bag, slit end to end as if by a knife, and his clothes and belongings scattered around the room.

"Dear God, please have mercy."

Noah heard the sound of Holly's voice praying behind him, and his own heart felt momentarily too stunned to put what he was thinking into words.

Then he saw the blood, fresh and red, pooling on the floor.

And he found the only words he could pray were *God, no... Please, no...*

NINE

"Seth!" He shouted his friend's name as loudly as he could. "Seth! Where are you?"

Tires screeched on the driveway outside as a vehicle slammed on its brakes.

Instinctively, Noah's arm shot around Holly, as he stepped in front of her, shielding her and pulling her to safety. He heard the sound of footsteps. A man was running across the parking lot toward them. Noah pressed them back against the wall.

"Seth!" Liam burst through the door, then froze. His face paled. His eyes turned to Noah. "Noah! What are you doing here? Where's Seth?"

"I don't know where Seth is," Noah said. "He called me and told me to come here. I arrived, found the place trashed, a lot of blood and no Seth."

He watched as a prayer crossed Liam's lips, then felt Holly step out from behind him. Liam blinked, and Noah watched as he took in her new look in a glance.

"Who's this?" Liam asked. "What's she doing here?"

"It's Holly," Noah said. "Guess you could say she's in disguise."

And even though it's not my place to ask, I'd very much like it if you stopped staring at her.

"Where were you?" Noah demanded, with more bite in his voice than he liked. "Why weren't you watching Seth?"

"You know where I've been," Liam said. "I've been digging into every possible lead I can find and coordinating with Mack and Jess."

"You shouldn't have left Seth alone!" Noah's voice rose even more. He felt Holly's hand brush his arm, not like she was trying to calm him down or shut him up, but trying to let him know he wasn't alone.

"You know he didn't want to be babysat!" Liam's pained voice matched Noah's in volume and intensity, and Noah could tell his old friend was aching every bit as much as he was. "It's not our role. We're detectives, not babysitters! I gave him the choice of coming with me. He didn't take it. He said he was chasing down a lead and very close to finding something."

Well, it looked like the Imposters had found him first. For a moment Noah stood there frozen, surrounded by the remains of the belongings of a man he'd promised to protect. *If only Seth had let me protect him.*

"It's not your fault," he told Liam at last. "He had this stubborn streak, doing things his way and only accepting help on his own terms."

"We gotta go," Holly interjected. She squeezed his arm again, harder this time, and her touch seemed to snap him back to the present. "I think the building's on fire."

And suddenly it was like everything hit his senses at once—the pervasive smell of gasoline, the tickle of acrid smoke in the back of his throat, the growing heat on his skin. And then he heard distant sirens.

They turned and ran out of the building. He reached the truck and looked back. Flames licked at the back windows of the hangar. The sirens grew louder.

"They set the building ablaze and called the fire department," Holly declared. "I don't know why. To destroy evidence. To trap us. All of the above."

He glanced back, watching the flames lick higher and higher as they moved through the building. Any moment now and they would reach the office. He prayed that Seth was safe.

"Let's swap vehicles," Liam said quickly. Noah felt him press the keys of his black SUV into his palm. "Get Holly to safety. I'll stick around here and see what I can find out about Seth."

Noah's hand clasped on his friend's shoulder. "But the building's on fire, which means that either the Imposters are here and set the fire, or they did it remotely and are on their way."

"Yup!" Liam said. "Divide and conquer. I'll buy you some time to get away. Then I'll get to Ottawa, meet up with Mack and Jess, and we'll strategize from there."

And Seth? And what about Seth? Would his body turn up in the rubble? Would his face appear in the next Imposters video about the auction?

Anguish filled Noah's heart. They'd come so close to a lead. Now they had nothing, and his friend was gone.

The sirens grew louder still. He could see the flashing lights of fire trucks on the horizon.

"Go!" Liam said. "I've got this. You take care of Holly!"

"Okay." Noah glanced at Holly's face.

She nodded, then started running around to the passenger side of Liam's vehicle. "Find out what happened to Seth!" she called.

"I will!" Liam shouted. "Stay safe!"

"You, too!" Noah bolted for the vehicle and leaped inside. Fire trucks were pulling down the narrow road now, blocking their exit. He glanced from the flashing lights to Holly, buckled his seat belt and started the engine. "Hold on. This might get rough."

"Isn't it always?" she said.

Yeah, pretty much. He gunned the vehicle toward the trucks, swerving in between them like a kid trying to win at bumper cars. Horns honked. Lights flashed. Sirens blared. He set his jaw and drove, ignoring the signals to slow down and weaving through the oncoming vehicles. Suddenly a dirt trail, narrow and snow-covered, appeared to his right. He swerved hard and aimed for it, flinging the SUV off the road and down the track. A field stretched in front of him. The SUV shook as they bounced across it, finally coming out onto a rural road. He glanced back. Lights flashed in the distance.

"I counted eight fire trucks, two ambulances and three cop cars," Holly said. "My guess is the Imposters called in the fire before they set the building alight. I expect they're now going to pop out from somewhere dressed as firefighters, paramedics or police, and mingle in the crowd."

Yeah, he suspected that, too. He prayed for Liam's safety and that Seth was still alive. Then he felt Holly reach over and squeeze his hand. He glanced her way, and saw her eyes were closed and a silent prayer seemed to be on her lips, before she opened them again and let go.

The road spread out before them, empty and straight. He slowed the engine.

"Sorry for driving like that," Noah said. "That's pretty much the exact opposite of how I promised Anne I'd drive."

"I won't tell her if you don't," Holly said.

"How's your head?" he asked.

She frowned. "Not great. But not as bad as it was three days ago."

He'd take it.

"You definitely break a lot of traffic laws for someone who's such a stickler for keeping the rules," she said.

He chuckled. "Hey, if you were paying attention you'd have noticed I signaled every lane change."

"Let me guess," she said. "You've never been in an accident."

"I'll have you know I got into my very first accident the day I bought my first vehicle."

"Really? I don't believe it."

"It's true," he said. "When I was seventeen years old, I bought a truck. It was four-wheel drive, a total beast and secondhand. I started working landscaping jobs when I was fourteen and saved up for years to buy it. My dad and mom gave me this whole lecture about safe driving, and I promised them I'd obey every traffic law."

"And?" she asked.

"And traffic laws don't apply off-road." He grinned. "I took it up a hill near my house, drove it through a grove of trees, scratched off the paint, tore out the transmission and hit a rock so big it bent the front axle. I had to hire a tow truck to loop a chain around it and basically pull it down the hill."

Holly snorted. Yeah, he could see now it was funny.

"I was without a vehicle for months after that. Sunk all my money and spare time into trying to fix it."

"And how did your dad and mom handle it?" she asked.

He laughed. "They weren't happy, but they didn't punish me. They just made sure I faced the consequences of my actions."

He frowned. And hadn't that been what his life had been built around? The idea that actions had consequences and people had to face them? That life offered no cheat codes or shortcuts, and that bad things happen when people didn't own up to what they'd done.

His phone buzzed. He dug it out and glanced at the screen. It was Liam. He'd made it out safely, hadn't seen any sign of Seth and was now on his way to meet up with Mack and Jess. *Regroup.* That's all they'd done since this had started. Run and regroup. Run again and regroup again.

Noah glanced at the beautiful, strong woman sitting beside him, still with her crazy fluffy hood and superlong hair. Her makeup hadn't even smudged. His nephew was talented.

For a moment, Noah let himself just look at her, as all the things he couldn't do, had failed at or wished he could accomplish cascaded through his mind. If he gave up and sold the gym, he'd be able to use his share of the money to buy a house, pay off his credit card debts and be a responsible enough man to be with a woman like Holly. He wouldn't have a problem applying for higher level security clearance because Caleb wouldn't be his business partner, so the feds wouldn't be looking at the gym's unpaid bills or his brother's mistakes and gambling.

He'd been carrying this burden for so long and still didn't know the right thing to do. But somehow the idea of letting Caleb ruin himself felt unthinkable. Insurmountable problems hemmed Noah in on every side with no sign of a solution. But maybe he could start by admitting he had a problem, asking for advice and getting his head on straight before he went back to the farmhouse and talked it out with Anne.

"Holly?"

"Yeah?" She turned toward him, and again something leaped inside his chest. It was ridiculous, the impact she had on him. How was it even possible for someone to be so beautiful and not know it?

He took a deep breath.

"If it's okay with you, I'd like to make a brief detour before we go back to the house," Noah said. "I've been wrestling with a personal problem for a really long time and I could use some advice. It has nothing to do with the Imposters, the auction or any of that. It's about Caleb, Anne and the kids. I think I need help, and I'm hoping that maybe you can be the one to help me."

Bros Gym made a great first impression from the outside, Holly thought, with its huge parking lot and large glass windows on the main floor. Faded signs advertised squash courts, a basketball court, a pool, a dojo, a boxing ring, spin and aerobic classes, saunas, steam rooms, and on-site therapists and coaches of various kinds. Only the deserted parking lot and blank stares of the empty windows gave any sign it was closed.

"Welcome to my problem," Noah said. He pulled to a stop by the front door and cut the engine.

"You own this place?" Holly asked.

"Sixty percent of it," Noah said. He slipped from the SUV, then waited as she climbed out and followed him. "Caleb owns the rest. He was really into training here when he was younger. Helped him work out his aggression and attachment issues. He said it was the only place he felt at home. He talked the owner into giving him a job here when he was twenty. Worked here, doing everything from maintenance, to coaching, to eventually becoming the assistant manager by the time he was twenty-eight. When the owner retired, he told Caleb he wanted him to have it."

Noah punched a code in the keypad by the door, then pushed the door open and they stepped inside. The building was freezing. The smell of dust, old equipment and neglect filled her lungs. A handful of canned energy drinks still sat in the fridge behind the front desk. A single pair of long-forgotten sneakers lay on the shoe rack. Instinctively, Holly reached for the light switch, but he caught her hand.

"No power," he said. "Electricity and water were all cut off months ago when Caleb stopped making payments. Come on, I'll give you the tour."

"Lead the way." She squeezed his fingers gently, and somehow, as they walked toward the cold and dim exercise machine graveyard, she found herself not letting go of his hand. He didn't let go of hers, either.

They walked hand in hand, like children sneaking around a building at night, past the front desk, down the rows of exercise machines and toward the main hallway. Empty holes and wires pockmarked the walls where she guessed flat screen televisions had once been. Gaps lay in the rows of equipment, as if someone had taken a single machine and left the rest behind.

They walked down the corridor, past various training rooms, before coming out in a large central hall that contained the boxing area, punching bags and ring. He stopped, and they stood there for a long moment in silence.

"It's been years since I've been here," he said. "More years than I liked to remember. Caleb was still running it then. We argued about some business decisions he had made, then he kicked me out. The next time I drove up this way, the gym doors were locked and Caleb was gone. He'd gotten a job as a long-haul truck driver. He ran from this like he runs from everything."

"So, how did you end up buying it?" she asked, her voice a whisper in the darkened space.

"Caleb wanted to run this business more than anything," Noah said. "My parents gave him a rather generous inheritance and my mom suggested, pretty much on her deathbed, that I go into business with him as a silent partner. So I did."

Wintry blue light filtered in from windows at the side of the room. Dark gray and purple shadows crossed the floor at their feet.

"It's a really beautiful place," she said. "It's incredible."

He glanced around the room, then looked down at his hand still holding hers.

"It is," he said. "It could've been. You haven't even seen the second floor yet. But it was always Caleb's dream, not mine. All I really ever wanted was for Caleb to succeed. But he flaked on this, just like he flaked on everything else. And now…"

His voice trailed off.

"Anne wants you to sell it," she supplied.

To her surprise, something flashed in his eyes. Something bright, sharp and strong.

"Anne has found a buyer," he said. "Caleb is sick of this place and wants it gone. He hasn't paid the mortgage in months, so I've been paying it, along with catching up on the back utility and other bills he left."

"This is why you didn't go for that promotion?" She stepped back. "Because you don't want the scrutiny coming down on this investment? This is the financial liability you've got hanging around your neck…?"

"Partly," he admitted. "I know the size of the mortgage in relation to my income looks bad, especially with the past lack of payments and the fact that it's clearly not turning a profit. The bigger factor is that since Caleb and I are coinvestors in this place, they're going to take a big, hard look at him, too. And that's not a pretty picture. He doesn't want or need that scrutiny. While I don't think his record of personal mistakes and financial failings is necessarily going to stop me from getting my security clearance, they're still going to question if he has the potential to get me into financial jeopardy or compromise me legally, and I don't want that for him."

He dropped her hand, took a step back and swung his arms wide.

"But if you think I've lost money in this place, you're wrong," he said. "That's part of what makes the situation so nuts. This property has increased in value. The buyer Anne found will make us a very generous offer. They want to put a whole regional housing and recreational complex in here."

She gazed at him, searching his face. Then what was the problem? He'd invested in a business he hadn't wanted to be part of. His foster brother apparently didn't want anything to do with it anymore. The solution seemed so simple.

He lifted his gaze to the ceiling and Holly realized whatever he was going through was way deeper than ridding himself of an investment property.

"Then why not sell it?" she asked. "I don't get it."

"Do no harm." He said the words so softly she barely heard him.

"What?"

"Lord, may I do no harm." He looked over and the full strength of his gray eyes fell upon her face. "It's something my dad used to pray under his breath whenever he was struggling to deal with whatever challenges or pain the children they fostered came through our door with. Whatever tantrum they were throwing or invisible battle they were fighting right there, in my space, in my way, in the middle of our living room or kitchen, my dad would always pray for the same things. That we would do no harm. That we would show love, extend grace and offer mercy. Again and again, over and over, day after day, after day. Those were the words he lived by. That was the kind of man he raised me to be. He'd say we couldn't control, change or even know the pain people had faced before they came into our lives. But we could do our very best to love them.

"I invested in this property because I loved him, he was my brother, because he was the happiest, strongest and healthiest he'd ever been when he was training and exercising. And whenever he stopped exercising, it was like he deteriorated, fell apart. Without a purpose he didn't have the strength to be the man he wanted to be, for himself, for Anne or for the kids."

Noah stepped back again and once more raised his arms, like a maestro conducting an orchestra or a boxer celebrating a fight.

"So, I set conditions on the loan." His voice rose until it echoed in the room. "Things I wanted him to promise to do, if I was investing my life in him, even though I knew Caleb would hate me for it. But they were all things he'd said he wanted to do. He had to keep going to church. He had to keep getting counseling with Anne, to help them heal the fact that he'd left the marriage and come back, more than once. He had to keep taking business courses to finally get a diploma or a degree. He had to stop gambling once and for all."

Noah paused, stepped forward and took her hands again. "Not because I wanted to control his life," he said, "but because I loved him. Not because I was trying to save him, but because I wanted to help him save himself. I don't want anything to do with this place. I want to sell it. But if I do and he suddenly gets a windfall from the sale, I'm afraid he'll gamble it, squander it and wreck his life. I'm afraid he'll leave Anne and the kids with nothing. You don't give a drunk a bottle of whiskey, or cocaine to an addict. And I don't want to sell this place, watch Caleb destroy himself with his share of the money and know I could've done something to stop it. I feel so lost and that's why I'm telling you. Because you're smart, savvy and driven. Because I like you. I respect you. I trust you. And I'd really like to hear your opinion."

She pulled him closer. Her heart seemed to clench in her chest.

"I don't know what you should do," she said. "Maybe if you wait six months, it'll be right to sell. Or maybe you could wait for years, and the situation would only get worse, and you'd find yourself wishing you'd done something a whole lot sooner. I just know you can't save him."

"I know." He said the words so softly she could barely hear them, and yet with a strength that felt like they were coming from somewhere very deep inside him.

"I get that you're the kind of guy who wants to save everyone," she said. "I really do. But you couldn't stop Seth from going rogue, you couldn't save everyone you grew up with and you can't even save every single person in witness protection. You can do your very best. But you don't always succeed."

"I know that, too," he said. "But somehow it really helps to hear it coming from you."

He looked down at their linked hands, then stepped

closer. So close that their clasped hands were the only thing between them.

"I'm going to hug you now," she said. "Okay?"

That grin she was beginning to really love turned up the corners of his mouth. "Okay."

She dropped his hands, stepped toward his chest, wrapped her arms around him and pulled her to him. For a very long moment they just stood there in the empty gym that had somehow swallowed up his life. She closed her eyes and pressed her cheek against his chest and listened to his heartbeat. Then she pulled back, just enough that she could tilt her head up and look in his face.

"I like, respect and trust you, too," she said. "Just for the record."

He chuckled. "Thank you."

"You can't save me, either," she said. "I know you want to. And I really, really appreciate that you do. Not a lot of people have ever tried or wanted to save me. But you can't just roll me up in Bubble Wrap or tissue paper and keep me safe, any more than you can reach into the back of my head and fix the concussion. The best you can do is..."

Her words trailed off. What had she been about to say? The best he could do was what, exactly? She didn't want to let herself think the words. Instead, she let her hands slide up around his neck. He pulled her closer until she could feel his heart beating into her core.

"I can have your back," he said, softly.

"Yeah." Her lips were so close to his now it would take so little to reach up and kiss him. "And you can talk to me about your problems. And you can hug me."

"Can I kiss you?" he asked.

Should he? No, that was a foolish idea. They shouldn't kiss. He knew it and she knew it. It was reckless and risky and only going to lead to a very painful goodbye.

But could he kiss her? Yes. Absolutely. Very much, yes.

She slid her fingers into his hair, tilted his face down toward hers and answered his question by letting her lips brush his. They kissed each other, gently and sweetly in the dying light. It felt right, being there in his arms, with his hands on her back and her fingers on his neck. He felt like strength, safety and home. He felt right in a way that nothing had ever felt right before.

Sudden bright and glaring light flooded the room, with the snap and pop of dozens of fluorescent bulbs springing to life at once. She leaped back, raising her hands instinctively into a fighting stance.

Noah had said the building had no power. Why was there light?

"Okay, I've got to admit I did not see this coming." A voice came from the balcony above. She blinked and looked up. Seth was leaning over the railing of what looked like an exercise studio. "So, is it true that you two are getting married?"

TEN

"What are you talking about?" Noah felt the words flying from his mouth like bullets as he turned and strode to the staircase that led up to the second floor. Before he could run up the steps, he saw Seth coming down them. "How are you alive? And what are you doing here?"

Seth stopped a few steps from him and raised his hands defensively. "Hey! Whoa! I thought you'd be a lot happier to see me alive!"

"I'm ecstatic to see you alive!" Noah shouted. He strode back to the boxing ring where he'd left Holly, leaving Seth hurrying after him. "I'm thrilled. I'm doing a veritable happy dance inside. Really I am. But I'm also really, really frustrated. Maybe even a little bit angry."

He turned back, then paused, so Seth wouldn't feel crowded or hemmed in. Noah couldn't remember the last time he'd admitted he was angry or let words like that slip from his lips. But something about admitting his fears to Holly, kissing her and holding her in his arms, had jarred something lose in him.

"Go ahead." Noah crossed his arms. "Tell me what happened. Why was there blood all over the safe house?

Why was everything smashed? Why are you here? Why are the lights working?"

"They found me!" Seth's voice rose. "The Imposters traced me. I found a lead online to locating Snitch5751 and they used it to find me."

"What's the lead?" Holly asked.

"A Wi-Fi network name," Seth said. "Now all we have to do is figure out whose Wi-Fi network that is and we'll know where Snitch5751 was when he contacted the Imposters. But that's like finding an electronic needle in a global haystack. I'm doing an online search for it and the algorithm hasn't come up with a solution yet. But once we find it, it'll show us where exactly Snitch5751 was located when he messaged the Imposters about Holly. But apparently it was enough for them to find me. Gotta tell you there's nothing scarier than spying on your enemy's online traffic and seeing a GPS route to your current location. So I destroyed what I could, trashed the place and ran."

"And the blood?" Noah's arms crossed tighter.

"I had some on me," Seth said. "It was in my emergency pack in case I ever needed to fake my death in a pinch and disappear off the grid. And really, considering some of the other stuff I've dropped so far in this conversation, I'm surprised you're focusing on that."

Did he mean the wisecrack about Noah and Holly getting married? Yeah, he was going to ignore that.

"Seth," Noah said. "I put my life on the line, multiple times, to save yours and keep you alive. And you don't trust me. You keep things from me. You make my job harder. I get where you're coming from, I really do. I get that trust is near impossible for you, considering everything you've gone through, and I don't blame you for that. But…"

His voice sputtered. He couldn't find the words. Why couldn't he find the words?

"But it hurts," Holly said. Her voice came from behind him, gentle but strong, and he felt a warmth move through him. He heard her cross the floor. "Maybe that's not the word Noah would've chosen, and I'm not going to put words in his mouth, but not being respected and trusted hurts."

Then he felt her hand brush his arm and close over his biceps.

"And I think Seth does respect you, Noah," she said. "Even if he doesn't say it and is lousy at showing it. He faked his death. He could've dropped off the grid and gone his own way. But instead, he came here." Then he felt her pull her hand away. "Also, apparently he turned the power back on. Care to explain that?"

Noah turned back to Seth and didn't think he'd ever seen him look so chagrined.

"I found this place doing a search of you online," Seth said. "I emailed the utility companies and got the electricity and water turned back on when I realized we might need to hide. And Holly's right. I could've gone anywhere. But I didn't, I came here, because I really am thankful for everything you've done to help me. I really am."

Noah noticed he hadn't mentioned whose email address he'd spoofed to get the utilities turned back on. Seth stretched his hand out, and for a moment Noah thought he was actually going to try to hug him. Instead, his hand hovered in the air between them awkwardly, like he wasn't quite sure what to do with it.

Noah clasped it in an athlete's grip handshake. "Forgiven," he said.

"Now, why the wisecrack about us getting married? I know it's one of several false rumors you started about me online, but people don't actually believe I'm eloping with anyone, do they?" Holly asked, and for the first time Noah heard a twinge of worry in her voice. Surely it had been a stupid joke, right? But judging by the look on Holly's face, she was worried Seth's planting of fake bread crumbs online might've gotten out of hand.

"Apparently I'm not the only one spreading wedding rumors," Seth said. He held up his phone, showing a beautiful bright picture of two stick figures getting married beside a Christmas tree. "Little girl named Lizzy Reed drew a picture in her preschool class of her uncle getting married at Christmas."

"That's what I was afraid of," Holly said. "Drew said Lizzy's been telling everyone you're getting married."

Yeah, but that was nothing but childish prattle. Noah's heart stopped. "How did you get a copy of this?"

"A preschool volunteer posted it online," Seth said. "I've had a continual search running for anything related to Anne or either of you. It had a handful of likes and comments before I got to it, but nothing more than 'Aww' and 'Squeal!' I took it down instantly and crashed their server."

Noah ran his hand over his head. Taking Holly to Anne had seemed like the least bad option they'd had at the time. But this was too close a call. Maybe it was time they moved on.

"Do you think the Imposters saw it?" Holly asked.

"Very unlikely," Seth said. "They're probably looking for you under your legal name and have no idea you're anywhere near Keswick or linked to Noah."

"What do we know about the Wi-Fi address?" Holly asked.

"Nothing yet," Seth said. "It's just a string of letters and numbers."

He held it up on his phone. Holly whistled.

"I can tell you exactly whose Wi-Fi server that is." She glanced at Noah. "It's General Bertie's manor house. The one in the country where he holds his Christmas charity event. Whoever Snitch5751 is, he was on Bertie's property when he messaged the Imposters."

Noah felt his spine stiffen. "So this means that General Bertie is Snitch5715?"

But even if he wanted to stop Holly from testifying, why would he work with cyber terrorists? Why would he get them to kill Elias and steal the witness protection files?

"No," Seth said. "All it means is that someone was on Bertie's property and had access to his Wi-Fi network when he sent the message. He might have been framing the general for all we know. Now what we've got to do is find a way to access his network."

"What if you do the same thing the Imposters did?" Holly asked. "What if you steal one of his devices? Could you use his cell phone or laptop to access his network?"

"Yeah." Seth's eyes grew wide. "But we do that how?"

Holly glanced at Noah. "The Christmas charity gala. It's in two days and less than half an hour from here. I was in on the organizing of it. If you pull me a layout of the building I can strategize entrances, exits and security. All of it. I can get us in to grab to his device."

"Out of the question." Noah turned toward her. "You're not sneaking into General Bertie's party! I won't—"

As she watched he caught himself and stopped mid-sentence, his hand rising as if catching the words out of thin air. He swallowed hard and tried again.

"I don't like the idea," he said. "I think you sneaking into a place where everyone knows you, even looking different, is too risky. Even as strong and smart as you are. I know it's not my place to tell you what you can and can't do. I'm not pretending it is. I just think it's a foolish plan, and I don't like it."

She let out a long breath she hadn't even realized she was holding.

Well, that was a step up. She couldn't remember the last time someone had listened to her, taken her seriously and changed his or her mind without her having to fight tooth and nail for it. Something about it touched her heart in a way she couldn't put into words. It wasn't like the confusing, conflicting feeling of being wanted or desired. Or the warm soft feeling of being held in his arms. No, this was a stronger and more solid feeling. She felt respected.

"You're not wrong," she said. "It would be a huge risk."

The memory of the attack by the three masked men that originally pushed her to get into witness protection flickered across her mind. At the time she'd had the strength and the ability to fight them off. Would she now?

Okay, if he could grow, so could she.

"If I'm completely honest, I'll admit I don't know if I'm up to it," she said. "Don't get me wrong. I have no desire to be left behind. I'm the best asset you've got for this and I know if Seth gets ahold of the schematics I could at least give you some good intel on getting in and out of the building."

She looked at Noah and something seemed to flow between them, deeper than anything she could put into words.

"Okay," Seth said. "So, we dress up like the catering crew. Noah and I go in with trays of food while Holly stays in the van and coordinates with us through headsets."

"We're not dressing up as caterers," Noah said.

"Members of a private security firm they're using, then? Or would it be military?" Seth's forehead wrinkled. "Yeah, sorry, I'm strictly a behind-the-screen kind of guy. I've hit the limit of my movie heist clichés. Although I vaguely remember some movie where they hid behind a giant bunch of balloons?"

Holly chuckled and rolled her eyes. She turned back to Seth.

"None of the above," she said. "General Bertie gives away hundreds of turkeys and Christmas hampers to members of law enforcement. It's part of his community outreach and what makes him so beloved. There will be hundreds of people, in normal everyday clothes, lining up for food in the greeting line. I'm guessing you can get Noah's name on a list?"

Seth nodded. "Absolutely. Child's play. But I'm suggesting we go with a fake name. Maybe Mr. Smith?"

Noah chuckled. "Fine."

She felt her gaze narrow slightly. "You can pick a pocket, too, right?"

"I might be able to." Seth chuckled. "But I probably won't need to. I can stay in the car and hack into his local network, if I'm close enough. Although getting his laptop or phone would be amazing because it would help me get a data dump. Just grab it, I'll copy it and we'll put it back. We don't even have to steal it."

Holly glanced at Noah and once again it was like his gaze grabbed on to her and held on tight.

"So, we do that?" she asked. "You'd have probably been invited to the event anyway, right? And nobody knows you've been helping me. Yeah, taking Seth with us will be a pretty big risk. I'm sure Drew can help tweak his appearance. What do you think?"

"I like it," Noah said. "Okay, we do that."

She smiled. "Deal."

Could it really be so simple? She thought of all the fights she'd witnessed between her parents, and awkward, long-drawn-out pauses in conversation when they'd start arguing, not resolve the topic and then come back to it hours, days or even weeks later. They'd slowly pick at their arguments over time instead of just getting it out and over with.

Was it possible settling disagreements between two equally strong-willed people didn't have to be that way?

Two days later, it took over an hour for Drew to complete Seth's transformation. His signature shaggy, dirty-blond locks were shorn into a military, boy-next-door crew cut that Drew then dyed a light brown. Wearing a suit jacket borrowed from Noah, the hacker looked like any number of the police officers and military personnel who'd be at the gathering. A fact he was still complaining about bitterly from the back seat of the SUV as it wove its way through the dazzling, unbelievable array of lights surrounding Bertie's home. Elaborate Christmas displays of animals, soldiers and cascading fountains lined the long driveway to the manor house.

"You wanted a disguise," Noah said. He glanced over his shoulder from the driver's seat. "And it'll grow back."

Then Noah glanced sideways at Holly, his laughter fading but his smile deepening. He reached over and squeezed her hand. "You doing okay?"

Was she? She wasn't sure. Her fingers brushed slowly over his. Her eyes rose to her reflection in the sun visor mirror and the stranger looking back at her. Drew had fluffed her hair out even more, and done something with different colors of makeup and some kind of putty that made her cheeks look more angular and changed the entire shape of her face. Her fake turquoise eyes shone unnaturally. She looked nothing like herself. She'd been behaving nothing like herself recently, either. Or at least a lot less like herself than she'd have wanted to. She missed her short hair and clean face. She missed the comforting feel of her uniform. She missed waking up at the crack of dawn to serve her country.

She missed being herself more than she'd ever missed anyone.

Holly pulled her hand slowly from Noah's, turned her eyes toward the window and watched the beautiful, dazzling light displays as they inched by. Yet somehow, all she could see was Noah's reflection behind her, mingling with hers in the darkened window.

She'd started falling for a man who in turn was attracted to a Holly who wasn't fully her.

"So, does Noah know what Christmas is, Holly?" Seth asked.

She blinked at her reflection in the mirror. "My birthday? Yeah."

"You should do something to celebrate it," Seth said. "Get a cake."

"When all this is done," she said. "When life is back to normal."

When she was herself again, when she had her life back and when she no longer had to pray that hundreds of people weren't going to wake up on her birthday knowing the person from their past who'd caused them the most pain had bought their new identity online and was coming for them.

"Now people are going to park their cars," she said, "and walk over to the gatehouse for apple cider and cookies." She'd stay in the SUV with Seth, keep the engine running and stay connected to Noah through the tiny walkie-talkie earpiece Drew had hidden in her hair. "Keep me posted, okay?"

"Will do." Noah backed the vehicle into a spot near the end of the lot, with its nose pointing toward the exit. "If you see any sign of trouble, you get out of here. Okay? Don't wait. Just do whatever you need to do to get yourselves somewhere safe."

She nodded and didn't answer. Anne may have given her permission to drive again, but that didn't mean she was about to run away from danger and leave Noah behind.

He cut the engine and reached for her. His fingers brushed against her cheek. "Stay safe, okay? I don't want anything happening to you."

"I'm not planning on doing something stupid," she said. "I promise. Don't worry. I have a walkie-talkie in my ear and Seth will be tracking your location GPS. And yes, before you ask again, my head is fine. Now, go."

Noah hesitated another moment, like he was debating if he should try to hug her or give her a quick kiss goodbye. But no, she couldn't risk it. Knowing there was no place for him in her world and for her in his was hard enough.

Noah pulled back and swallowed hard, as if readjusting the words in his mouth before speaking them. "I've got something for you," he said. He reached into his ankle holster and pulled out a gun. It was a Glock 43 nine millimeter, and smaller than her normal service weapon, but as she took it from his grasp there was something comfortable about how it sat in her hand. "It's Anne's. She's a licensed gun owner and wanted you to have it, when I thought you were ready. But I'm really hoping you won't have to use it."

"Don't worry," she said, "I won't drop it."

A grin turned up his lips. "I never suggested you would."

He strode toward the reception. She waited a few seconds, then got out of the vehicle, intending to just to walk around to the driver's seat. But instead, somehow, she found herself standing alone in the parking lot, watching Noah's back as he walked toward the event, followed the path of glowing lights to the building and then disappeared inside. Dark trees festooned in glowing red and green bulbs surrounded the area. The building ahead shone with golden lights. Men and women got out of vehicles from the other side of the lot and started toward the building. She recognized a few of them, even at a distance, and imagined there were probably several more she'd know if only they turned her direction. She wondered how many would recognize her. None, she imagined.

Her eyes rose from the dazzling Christmas trees to the dark sky above.

Help me, Lord. I feel like I've found an incredible man who's worth risking my heart for, but have completely lost who I am.

Two sharp raps came from the window behind her. She glanced back at Seth, still sitting in the back seat of the SUV. His worried eyes met hers. "We've got company."

"Where?" Her hand snapped to Anne's gun as she scanned the lot.

"On this Wi-Fi network," Seth said. "Somebody else is trying to hack the same network I am. It's like they realized I was coming and tried to get here first to download everything they could access and then wipe it clean."

She closed her eyes and prayed, while she reached for the walkie-talkie button to alert Noah.

"Hey! Is there a problem?" His voice crackled in the earpiece before she could even push the mic button to speak to him, and she knew in an instant from his tone the answer to his question was yes.

She glanced instinctively toward the house.

"Don't move!" The voice speaking to him was rough, coarse and familiar.

The back of her head began to pound.

"Who are you?" This second voice was high and thin. "What's your connection to Corporal Asher?"

She turned back to Seth and his terrified eyes met hers through the window.

Time froze as she waited to hear what Noah would do, her heart aching as she anticipated his response. Instead, she heard the sizzle and pop of a stun gun and the thud of a body landing on the floor.

"John Smith," the Ghoul said, and she realized they must've found the fake ID Drew had created in Noah's wallet. "What do you want me to do with him? Take him to the van?"

"Nah, take Mr. Smith upstairs," the Wraith said. "You interrogate him there while I deal with the server. Figure out who he is, what he's doing here and what happened to Hildegard Asher. If anyone asks, say he passed out drunk and we're giving him a chance to sleep it off."

"Will do."

The memory of their faces might've been a blur, but those voices would haunt her nightmares for years It was the Imposters and they had Noah.

She glanced back at Seth. "I'm going in!"

His face paled even more, so ashen it was almost gray. "You promised Noah you'd stay in the car!"

"No, I promised him I wouldn't do anything foolish!" She yanked the door open and shoved the keys into his hand. "Leaving him to get tortured by a couple of evil criminals is definitely foolish!"

"What do I do?" Seth's voice rose in panic.

"Get behind the wheel," she said. "Keep hacking the Wi-Fi. Grab everything you can off Bertie's server to help us determine who Snitch5751 is. Let Liam, Mack and Jess know what's going on. Call in the authorities and let them know the Imposters have infiltrated General Bertie's charity Christmas gala. And please don't drive away and leave us here, unless someone runs up to the car and you think something bad's about to happen. Then floor it."

"You're going to get yourself killed!" Seth said.

"Maybe," she said. "Hopefully not. But this isn't about me. Or Noah. It's about the hundreds of lives that are going to be destroyed if this auction goes live."

She ran for the tree line, away from the path the guests were still taking, sprinting as quickly as she dared along the rows of colored lights, watching the snow turn from red to green at her feet.

Thankfully, Noah's earpiece was still transmitting, enough to let her know the Imposters were now carrying him up to the second floor. They hadn't found his microphone yet, but she was sure it wouldn't be long until they did. *Right, Lord, now what?* She reached the far side of the house and stood in the darkness against the wall, away from the lights and the noise of the gathering. Now what? Even with a disguise she couldn't just walk in the front door. Light shone down from above, spilling over a stone balcony. She glanced at the rock wall, felt the stones, and her fingertips brushed the space between them. She glanced up.

I can do it, Lord. I'm sure I can. Please, keep me from falling.

"I'm going downstairs," the Wraith said. "Wait until the music starts and then wake him up."

There was a grunt, a string of swear words and then her earpiece went dead. Looked like they'd found Noah's device. She wasn't going to wait. *God, please have my back.* She dug her fingertips in, gritted her teeth and started climbing, slowly feeling for hand- and footholds, ignoring the pain pounding through her head0 and praying with every breath.

She reached the balcony, grabbed the edge and tumbled over. For a moment she just lay there, panting and waiting for the pain to clear. Then she heard the strains of string instruments filtering up from the floor below. The music had started.

She dragged herself to her feet and stumbled toward the nearest sliding glass door. The latch was locked, but she forced her shoulder into the frame and popped it free. She tugged the door open and stumbled through, into a study, holding Anne's gun at the ready.

A man rose from behind the desk, grabbing for a weapon as he did so. He was elderly, nearing seventy, with a full white beard and a firm, unwavering stance that told her he would put his ability to pull a trigger up against hers any day.

It was General Bertie. The man she was testifying against. The reason she was in this whole mess.

"Drop your gun!" he ordered.

"General, listen to me." She risked a step forward. "Please. I'm not going to hurt you. The Imposters have infiltrated your party and I need your help to stop them and save a good man's life."

ELEVEN

It was a standoff. Holly stood in the study, keeping her weapon trained on the general even as she stared down the barrel of his gun.

"Who are you?" he started. She watched for a second as the question hovered on her former mentor's lips. Then something clicked behind Bertie's eyes. He nodded. "Corporal Asher."

"Yup," she said. She tightened her grip on the gun. "Please, put down your weapon, sir. I'm not going to hurt you. I just want to stop some criminals and save some people."

The general didn't move. The music below grew louder. Her heart ached.

Lord, please be with Noah and keep him safe until I can find him.

"Drop your gun, Corporal."

"I can't do that," she said. "I'm sure you've heard of the Imposters. They're cyber criminals who've stolen the entire RCMP witness protection database and are about to auction it off online tomorrow unless we stop them. Now two men, one big and one small, dressed in some kind of uniform that implied they belonged here, just carried a man upstairs. He will be tortured if I don't stop him. Please let me go find him."

Bertie's head shook. He didn't believe her. He thought she was standing there, making up lies. "I'll do no such thing! I don't know why you're really here, but you will put down your weapon and get off my property before I have you arrested!"

"No! Listen to me—"

"Asher!" His voice was sharp and direct, with the tone she'd followed so many times, automatically. "There is no need for any of this. All I want is an opportunity to testify honestly before the inquiry and clear my reputation. I'm sorry you decided to go this route and try to make a name for yourself with cheap theatrics and lies. But whatever game you think you're playing, it stops here and now."

"You bartered away weapons to the local warlord families, which they then used to slaughter innocent people!" Her voice rose. She didn't know if she was going to be able to dissuade him from turning her in and convince him to help her find Noah before it was too late. But succeed or fail, she was done holding back any punches. "I don't care what your motivation was! I don't care what story you told yourself to make that okay! You betrayed your country. You betrayed the mission. You betrayed everything you taught me we believed in! You betrayed me!"

Her voice broke as, to her surprise, hot tears filled her eyes. Suddenly she found the words she'd never thought she'd say stumbling unexpectedly from her mouth.

"I looked up to you, General," she said. "I respected you and served faithfully under you. When I stepped forward to tell the truth—a truth you refused to tell—you did nothing to stop your defenders from coming after me, threatening me, blackballing me and trying to silence me." Her voice broke. "Did you know three men came after me, trying to stop me from testifying against you? Three criminals, hired by someone who claimed to be defending you, attacked me just to shut me up!"

Bertie's face reddened. "I had nothing to do with that!"

"You heard about it, though, didn't you?" she asked. "And you did nothing to stop it! You did nothing to stop people from trying to harass me into silence. Someone who went by the handle Snitch5751 arranged my attack, the death of Detective Elias Crane of the RCMP, the theft of the witness protection files—all of it—from this Wi-Fi address. And if you'd just put your gun down, let me find the undercover detective I'm working with and let investigators search your devices, we could stop him and figure out who he is. Unless the fact that you're standing here, holding me at gunpoint, means that it was you. And you've been behind all of this all along."

"I assure you, I did no such thing!"

"Then prove it!" Her voice rose again. "Be a better person than this! Be the person everyone downstairs thinks you are. Who I thought you were. Tell me where my friend is! Help me find him! If you want to get me arrested for breaking and entering and threatening you, fine! Just be the man you claim to be, stop these criminals and let me save my friend's life."

She gasped a breath, feeling her head pound and

emotion surge through her brain. Tension crackled through the air.

"Drop the gun, Corporal, and I'll take you to your friend," he said, his voice as firm as steel. "I imagine he would be the Mr. Smith I hear you're marrying?"

She didn't answer. Just how effective had Seth's online rumor mill been?

"I'm having you both arrested," he continued, "filing a restraining order against you and petitioning to have you banned from testifying against me on account of your clear personal vendetta and instability. As for the rest of your ridiculous story, you can tell it to the authorities."

She raised her hands and let the gun drop to the floor.

"Hands on your head," he said. "Fingers linked."

Lord, I really hope I'm doing the right thing right now. But what other choice do I have?

She did as he asked. Bertie let out a sigh, then gestured to a door in the side wall that she'd thought was a cupboard.

"I saw the man you may be describing passed out, apparently drunk, being escorted and carried by two of the catering team—"

"They're criminals," she said quickly. "They're behind the witness protection auction. They'll torture and kill him. I'm not lying. You have to believe me—"

"They took him into a lounge at the end of the hall," he went on, talking over her. "I'm not about to walk the key witness against me through an event at gunpoint, so we're going to go through the back. You're going to walk in front of me, nice and slowly. Got it?"

Yeah, she got it. She walked where he indicated and

felt him press the gun into the back of her head. The thought of spinning around, fighting back and battling for her life against the man who'd ruined it rose up inside her. But all that mattered right now was finding Noah. Even if all she could do after this was sit in a jail cell, praying that the Imposters were caught and that Seth, Liam, Mack and Jess had stopped the auction.

"Open the door," he said. "Nice and slow."

She did. They walked forward into another office and crossed through it, to a door on the other side. She opened that second door and saw Noah.

He was sitting in a chair, facing the wall to her right. The Ghoul stood behind him with a gun pressed to the back of his head. Cold air whipped at them through the open patio door. And then it was as if everything happened faster than she could think. Sirens sounded outside. The fire alarm screeched. Water poured down from the sprinklers in the ceiling. The Ghoul turned, his gun rose and Noah shouted at her to get down.

A bullet flew. And she watched as the Ghoul shot General Bertie.

Bertie fell to the ground, shouting in pain. Noah swung back, catching the Ghoul in the jaw and knocking the weapon from his hand even before he could think to fire again. Then Noah sprang to his feet, his eyes searching out Holly's face as she dropped to the floor beside the general. There was a crash behind him as the Ghoul knocked over a table, dived through the open door and out onto the balcony. In an instant, the criminal had vaulted over the railing and disappeared into the snowy yard below. The flashing lights and sounds of approaching emergency vehicles filled the air outside. And still, water from the sprinklers rained down around them.

"Holly!" In a heartbeat, Noah had crouched by her side. "Are you all right?"

"I'm okay." She clutched his hand, linking her fingers through his. "But Bertie's losing a lot of blood. Where's the Wraith?"

"I don't know," Noah said. "I only saw the Ghoul when I came to."

The sirens grew louder. Water soaked their skin. His teeth chattered. By the sounds of things, guests were streaming from the building below. The two of them could find a way to slip out the back without being seen.

"Before you ask, I dropped the gun," Holly said. "It was the only way to save your life."

"We've got to leave," Noah said. "We can go through the back hallway and climb down from a different balcony."

He tried to pull her to standing. But she clutched his hand and held on tight.

"Not without General Bertie," she said. "We need to get him to paramedics immediately. I don't know if he has anything to do with the Imposters or Snitch5751 or not. But either way, I'm not about to just let him die." As he watched, she slid the man's body over her shoulder and tried to stand. "You need to carry him. I can't."

He blinked. "He ruined your life."

"Yeah! Now help me save his!"

Seriously? There was so much on the line and she was insisting they risk their lives to save that of the man who was behind several crimes and might be behind more. Her eyes met Noah's, fierce, brave and every bit as stubborn as he was. And his heart swelled as he realized how unbelievable she was. In another time and another place, he'd have given anything to have a woman like her by his side.

"Okay, fine." He dropped to one knee and turned to the general, whose eyes were open, though his face was pale. "Excuse me, sir, but I'm going to have to lift you."

Noah slid his arms underneath the old man and lifted him in a fireman's carry.

"Look on the bright side," Holly said. "Now we both know what at least one of the Imposters looks like! So we'll have no trouble finding a paramedic to trust."

Yeah. His body was still tingling and sore and smarting from whatever jolt of electricity they'd shot through him. It had been much stronger, more painful and longlasting than any legal stun gun. And then they'd topped it up by shoving some kind of drug-soaked handkerchief in his face that had made him drowsy. And now he was carrying the bloody body of the man who'd put Holly through all the pain, fear, recovery time and anguish Noah had watched her go through. He was risking both their lives to carry this man to safety. Because Holly had asked him to and it was the right thing to do.

"Come on," Noah said. He stood up taller and steadied Bertie on his shoulders. "Let's do this."

They pushed through the study door and out into the hallway, feeling the cascading sprinklers pounding on their skin and following the flowing water as it streamed down the stairs. The blaring scream of the fire alarm sounded around them, blending into a cacophony of noise with the sirens outside and the babble of people fleeing the building. He burst out the front door and immediately felt the wintry air start freezing his clothes to his skin. He made a beeline through the crowd and the chaos toward an ambulance.

"Help!" He ran up to a pair of paramedics, who were flanked by a uniformed female cop, wishing he could flash his badge, but knowing until Snitch5751 was discovered it wasn't safe. "General Bertie Frey has been shot and needs immediate medical attention."

The paramedics scrambled, helping the elderly man off his shoulders and onto a stretcher. Noah grabbed an emergency blanket from an outstretched arm.

"Who shot him?" The red-haired female detective was to his right.

"One of the Imposters," he said. "They're the urban terrorists behind the theft of stolen witness protection files and the threatened release of them tomorrow."

And probably long gone by now.

"Holly?" He turned back, clutching the blanket, and for a moment panic welled up inside him when he couldn't spot her. He ran back through the crowd, pushing past upset party guests and emergency personnel. "Holly! Where are you?"

Then he saw her. She was huddled on a bench by the edge of the parking lot, with her arms wrapped around her skull and her head buried deep in her hood. He ran to her, dropped to his knees in the snow and pulled the blanket around her. She lifted her head to look at him, and his heart ached to see the pain in her eyes.

"Let me guess," he said softly, feeling something catch in his chest. "Your head hurts?"

"Yeah." The faint glimmer of a smile floated on her

lips. "I've really got to start taking a break from flashing lights and sirens. They're not great for concussions. Thankfully, my coat and boots are waterproof. But I can barely feel my legs." She closed her eyes for a moment and he watched as pain crossed her face. Then she let her hands drop to her lap. "How's Bertie?"

"With the paramedics." He grabbed both her hands in his. "Come on, let's get you out of here."

She stood, and he found himself wrapping his arm around her as they started across the parking lot to the SUV. The sounds of honking filled the air. The lot was jammed with cars trying to leave. Then he realized a single vehicle was sitting in the middle of the exit as if waiting for something and forcing all others to go around it. It was Seth.

Noah reached the car and climbed in the back seat with Holly. Seth's worried eyes met his through the rearview mirror. "You're alive. That's a good thing."

"Yup," Noah said. Thanks to Holly coming after him.

Seth hit the accelerator and the SUV lurched forward. "I get now why not telling you I was alive before was a bad thing."

"I'm guessing you set off the fire alarms and called in the emergency?"

"Yeah." Seth blinked. "You're wet."

"Yeah, that's what happens when you set off the sprinklers."

"Sorry."

"Just pump up the heat."

"Did you manage to grab a laptop?" Seth asked.

"No, we were kind of busy," Noah said. "Did you hack into the Wi-Fi?"

"I did," Seth said, "and I downloaded everything I could, but Snitch5751 wasn't anywhere connected to the network. If I had to guess, I'd say he wasn't at the party."

Did that mean Snitch5751 wasn't General Bertie?

"Now what?" Seth asked.

"Drive," Noah said. "Slowly. Back to the farmhouse, but take back roads and detours, and keep an eye out for anyone following us."

Noah slid his arm around Holly's shoulders. She was quiet and shut down, like she'd slipped deep inside herself and was hiding there. He cradled her to his side, feeling the comfort of having her there. She nestled against him, letting her head fall onto his chest, as Seth drove. And as cold, uncomfortable and worried as Noah was, something inside him wished the drive would never end.

The house was quiet when they reached it. Anne helped Holly inside and upstairs. Seth sat down in a corner and started working again, his frantic tapping filling the small room like the ticking of a clock.

Noah paced, letting prayers pour through him.

Help me, Lord. What do I do? I care about this woman more than I've ever cared about anyone before. I don't know how to save her. I don't know how to protect her. I'm no closer to finding out who Snitch5751 is or his connection to Bertie. The witness protection identities auction is tomorrow, and I've never felt so helpless. Please, help me.

The grandfather clock sounded, again and again, until he'd counted twelve bongs. Seth's tapping froze. His eyes met Noah's. It was midnight. Christmas Eve had arrived.

The auction was today.

"So, what's the plan?" The sound of Holly's voice broke the tense silence. He looked up. She was coming down the stairs toward them, swathed in a simple gray track suit. The makeup was gone from her face, her hair was wrapped up in a towel and he knew without a doubt he'd never seen anything more beautiful in his life.

"I don't know," he said. "We've got twelve hours to find the Imposters and stop the auction."

And they were no closer than they'd been six days ago. Jess had monitored the situation from within RCMP headquarters, Mack had shaken every criminal tree he could find, Liam had called in every favor he had from every cop he'd ever served with and Seth had spent every possible minute online. They'd exhausted every plan they'd come up with and they were helpless to stop what was about to happen when the clock next struck twelve.

Holly reached the bottom step and crossed the floor toward him. She grasped his hand and held it, not saying anything but just being there.

They'd exhausted every strategy they'd brainstormed back in Seth's loft, except Holly's. She'd suggested baiting a trap and letting the Imposters come to them, but he'd brushed her off. And why? Because he'd thought he knew better? Because he was so focused on saving her he hadn't respected her need to help save herself?

"If it's not too late, I want to go with your original plan, Holly," he said. "I want to make the Imposters come to us. Here. Today."

"It's too late." Seth shook his head. "We suddenly announce where Holly is hiding, hours before the auction, and they'll never believe it isn't a trap."

"But what if we use bread crumbs that someone dropped days ago?" Noah asked. "Thanks to you, rumors have been swirling online for days that Hildegard Asher applied for a marriage license and the Imposters already think I'm John Smith."

Noah felt Holly squeeze his hand. "What are you doing?"

"Your plan," Noah said. He turned toward her. "We're going to bait a trap and lure the Imposters to us."

"But we can't…"

"Yes, we can," he said. "Because we already have the perfect cover. Something they won't even think is a trap. I'm sorry I didn't listen to you before. But let's go with your plan. Let's do this your way. Let's catch them today, this morning, before the auction goes live. Let's find an easily secured and remote location, hold a fake wedding and pretend to get married. What do you say?"

"No." Holly shook her head and pulled her hand away from his. "I won't do it. I don't want to pretend to marry you."

TWELVE

How could he do this to her? How could he so casually ask her to pretend that they were a couple, that they loved each other, that they wanted to spend their lives together? Noah's eyes were searching her face, looking puzzled, confused and even lost. She turned away. No, this was one step too far. All she'd done for days was pretend to be someone she wasn't, while developing very real feelings for this man. Pretending to marry him, pretending their relationship was something that it wasn't, was akin to pretending she didn't feel what she felt. No, worse than that, it was making a mockery of it. She couldn't pretend to be in love with a man she was beginning to fall in love with for real.

"Give us a second, Seth," Noah said. "Please."

She heard Seth get up, walk into the kitchen and close the door behind him. Then she stood there for a moment in the stillness of the farmhouse living room, listening to the sound of the snow pelting the windows outside, the clock ticking and her own beating heart.

"I feel like I should apologize," Noah said, after a long moment. "But I don't know why or what I did wrong."

"You don't need to apologize," she said. "You didn't do anything wrong."

"Then why aren't you looking at me?" His voice broke. "And why does my heart feel like someone is twisting it around like a dishcloth?"

She turned back. He was standing as close to her as he had been back at the gym when they'd kissed. It would take so little for her to lean forward and kiss him again. And somehow it felt wrong not to have his arms around her.

"I don't want to pretend to marry you," she said.

"Why not?"

"Because I don't want to pretend to have that kind of relationship with you."

"But why not?" He looked so lost. He didn't get it. How did he not get it?

"Why did you kiss me back in the gym?" she asked.

"Is that what I need to apologize for? I'm really sorry if I overstepped. I know I shouldn't have—"

"Don't say that," she said. "I don't need you to apologize for kissing me. I don't need you to apologize for anything." She paused. He didn't speak, and for a long moment she didn't, either. Then she grabbed his hands. "Tell me. Why did you kiss me, Noah?"

Because she knew why she'd kissed him. She'd kissed him because she wanted to. She'd kissed him because she liked him on more levels than she ever knew it was possible to like someone. She'd kissed him because he was kind, strong, caring and extraordinary.

And because he was the one and only man she wanted to kiss, every day, for the rest of her life.

She willed him to tell her that he felt the same way,

and that he didn't care so little for the thought of being with her that he was willing to fake the most important day of their lives.

"I don't know what to say, Holly. I don't understand," Noah said. "I thought you'd like the idea. I thought it's what you wanted. And again, I'm really sorry for kissing you. Clearly, I wasn't thinking."

She took a deep breath, stepped back and pulled her hands from his. Of course he didn't understand. They'd met only six days ago. They barely knew each other, and they'd been thrown together by circumstances beyond their control.

"The beauty of having a fake wedding is it's already been out there online for days," he said. "Seth already planted it and then the rumor grew online all on its own. The Imposters won't realize it's a setup. All we'd need is the team, a remote location with good lines of sight and no civilians. It just seems like such an easy solution. But if you can think of a better one, by all means let me know. I'm just focused on trying to stop the auction, and willing to do whatever it takes to save those lives."

She swallowed a painful breath. He was right. He was beyond right. People's lives were in danger. The auction was going live in less than twelve hours and she'd do whatever it took to stop it, too. She had to put the lives of the people in danger first. The fledgling feelings in her own ridiculous heart couldn't even begin to compare with that.

"No, you're right," she said. "We don't have time for another plan. I don't like this one, but I can't think of a better one."

He just stood there staring at her, hurt filling his

eyes, like he was drowning. She wanted to save him. She wanted to reach across the gap between them, open up her heart and make him understand how she felt about him and why. But she'd never opened her heart to anyone before. This wasn't the time or the place to start.

"Are you sure?" he said. "Because I don't want to push you into it if you're against it."

"There's no time." She ran her hand over her head, feeling the hidden wax keeping her fake hair in place. "Not for what we need to accomplish. You're right about choosing a remote location with no civilians. But we're not doing it in a church. I refuse to fake a wedding in a church."

He nodded. "Okay."

"Not the gym, either." She stepped back and crossed her arms. "I don't like it for a sting. Too many exists and entrances."

"Got it." He nodded again, but still looked so lost it wrenched something inside her. Why did he care so much? And if he cared, why couldn't he just come out and admit it? If she swam in to save him, they could both drown. "There's a one-room schoolhouse in town. It's owned by the historical society. It had good lines of sight and only one exit. I don't expect it's booked today."

She stepped even farther back. This was good. Keep focusing on practical aspects of the plan and block out the emotion. She could get through this. It was just like a military operation. But one with too many lies on the line.

"Can Seth make it look like it was booked days ago?" she asked. "But anonymously. Like we were trying to elope?"

Noah nodded. "I'm pretty sure he can."

"We also need to get Anne and the kids out of here," she said. "I don't want them anywhere near the Imposters. Not in the same town. Not in the same part of the province. Since as far as anyone will know you're John Smith, it shouldn't surprise anyone that they're not invited."

And as for her own family, fortunately her parents would never need to find out she'd had a fake wedding.

Noah glanced to the clock. "I can call Liam, Mack and Jess right now and get them here by sunrise," he said. "Mack can take Anne and the kids somewhere safe. She has friends in Barrie she can stay with. Liam and Jess can help put together a wedding. They've set up far more complicated undercover operations in a lot shorter time frames. Seth can make the online trail look real. Maybe it won't hold up to intense scrutiny, but they're not going to have a lot of time to look into it, if their plan is to kill us and still get the auction up by noon. We can set it up to look like a simple elopement. The story can be that we only met recently, it was love at first sight and we decided to get married. It fits the facts well enough and it's believable, especially considering your own parents only knew each other a few days before they decided to get married."

That was true. And the fact that he didn't know that was the exact worst thing he could've reminded her of right then just showed how little he actually knew her.

"Well, Anne's still up, so I'll go let her know the plan while you talk to Seth," Holly said. "I also suggest we both do a whole lot of praying."

She turned to go, then felt Noah's hand on her arm. She stopped, but didn't turn.

"Are you sure everything is okay?" he asked.

No, nothing was okay. It hadn't been in a long time and she didn't know when it would be again.

"My head is fine," she said, even though her heart wasn't. "All that matters is that we're going to do whatever it takes to catch the Imposters and stop the auction. They're not going to hurt all those innocent people. We won't let them."

And the foolish longing in her heart for an unforgettable man wasn't going to get in the way of that. She walked up the stairs without looking back, feeling her limbs shake with every step. She could do this. She knew who she was, she was strong and she was a soldier. She'd faced far tougher battles than this.

Then why did she feel scared in a way she never had before?

Anne answered her upstairs office door on the first knock. The doctor's keen eyes searched Holly's face. "What's wrong?"

"The auction goes live today at noon," Holly said. She stepped in and closed the door behind her. "We're hoping to make a last-ditch effort at stopping the Imposters by bringing them to us."

Anne sat and listened while Holly told her the plan.

"Okay," Anne said. "I'll make sure the kids are packed up and ready to go. Drew will probably want to help you get ready before he leaves. You can wear my old wedding dress. I gave it to Drew to make something out of. I think he's still awake and working on something."

Holly's heart thudded with a fresh horror. She hadn't even thought of what she was going to wear. "I can't wear your wedding dress."

"It's okay," Anne said. "It's just my first. I bought it secondhand, and Caleb and I have renewed our vows twice since then."

Twice? She had a hard enough time imagining a brilliant woman like Anne marrying Caleb once, let alone pledging herself to him three times. It was Christmas Eve and Caleb wasn't even here to be with his family. What was wrong with people in love? Her own mother had fallen in love with a man who she'd felt she had to give up her dreams for. Anne had fallen in love with a man who'd disappeared.

And I'm falling in love with Noah.

"What's wrong?" Anne asked.

"I hate everything about this plan," Holly said. "I hate weddings. My parents' marriage is a mess. They've been separated for years in this weird holding pattern where they're not together but haven't completely given up. And…"

Her voice trailed off.

"And between your parents' marriage and what you've heard about me and Caleb, the idea of getting married has left you with a pretty bad taste in your mouth?" Anne supplied gently.

Well, yes. But Anne's relationship was none of her business.

"I'm not marrying Noah," Holly said. "I'm pretending to marry a man named John Smith to lure cyber terrorists out into the open before a witness protection auction goes live."

Anne nodded.

"And even though it shouldn't, this whole situation

reminds me of my parents," Holly said. "They fell in love really fast."

"Caleb and I fell in love slowly," Anne said. "And several times, over many years and several breakups. I'd been very badly hurt, and he was the first man I knew who would never ever lay a hand on me. Sure, he'd run. But he would never hurt me. Caleb had been abandoned by everyone he'd ever loved. He needed someone who wouldn't give up on him, no matter how hard he ran. I'm not saying our marriage isn't broken, maybe beyond repair. But I still wouldn't trade anything for the good times we've had together."

"I know it's none of my business," Holly said. "I don't understand how you could do that."

"One day at a time," Anne said. "One prayer, one battle, sometimes even one breath at a time. Every love is as different as the two people in it. My relationship with Caleb is nothing like my parents' relationship was. Noah's parents had an incredibly strong, faithful and long-lasting marriage. And when Noah fully gives his heart to someone, he won't love that woman the same way that Caleb loved me. In my experience you just pray for the grace for the relationship you're in."

Holly nodded. Somehow that helped, but she didn't know why. As broken as Anne's heart might be, her love for Caleb was real, raw and built on the reality of trying to slog it out in life together. And no matter what Holly felt for Noah, when they walked down the aisle it would be nothing but pretend.

"Stop pacing, man!" Liam leaned forward and tapped Noah on the shoulder as they waited at the tiny wooden podium in the one-room schoolhouse. "I'm pretty sure your bride won't leave you at the altar."

"Har-har." Noah forced himself to chuckle. "Of course she wouldn't miss this mission for the world. The chance to catch the Imposters? Come on!"

The clock read ten o'clock. Setting the wedding two hours before the auction went live seemed like the perfect window of time. It was far enough from the start that the Imposters would justifiably feel they were able to stop the wedding, try to kill them and still be back online in time to ruin countless people's lives.

Everything had gone precisely according to plan. Liam, Jess and Mack had gotten to the house before the sun had risen. Mack had taken Anne and the kids to Barrie and made it back in time for the pretend wedding.

Now Liam stood behind the altar dressed in a suit to officiate the fake wedding, while Seth sat back at the farmhouse on the computer, looking for any sight of the Imposters online.

Noah brushed his hand against the microphone button in the pocket of his suit. "Any sign of trouble, Seth?"

"Nope," he answered. Noah heard tapping through the microphone. "All systems go, unfortunately. The auction countdown clock reads just a little over two hours. Lots of eager purchasers showing up in the online waiting room, ready to bid, and opening their secure lines to the auction. We got local criminals, international terrorists, organized crime and human traffickers. A virtual smorgasbord of evil."

All looking to get revenge and exploit victims' lives.

"How many are we talking?" Noah asked.

"Dozens," Seth said. "Over a hundred already. Looks like they're planning on rolling people's lives out one at a time."

An unsettled feeling brushed up Noah's spine. Why would people be online that early if the auction wasn't going to start for two hours?

"The countdown clock still says noon, right?" he asked.

"Yeah," Seth said. "No change there. Also, apparently bidding for each file starts at ten thousand dollars."

Noah's stomach turned. So that's how much they thought a human life was worth.

"You do realize there are hundreds of better-trained, better-equipped police officers and detectives spread out across the country right now, maybe even around the world, trying to stop this auction and take them down," Seth added. "It's kind of silly, when you think of it. They've got all that brain power and firepower, and here we think we're going to stop these guys with four regenerate detectives, a hacker, a whistle-blower and a fake wedding."

Yeah, it was, when he put it that way. After all, thanks to Jess's contacts and Drew's drawing abilities, the RCMP now had a pretty good sketch of the Ghoul based on Noah's and Holly's descriptions. Plus whatever security footage investigators had pulled from Bertie's party, not to mention the general's testimony. This little charade they were doing might be for nothing.

"Well, I for one am cheering for them," Noah said.

"I don't need this win. They can have it. I hope they take the Imposters down any second now."

He wasn't sure why his heart was beating so loudly at the moment. He just knew he didn't like it.

"And the bride has arrived!" Mack's voice crackled in his earpiece. "We're just pulling in now. No cars in the parking lot. Not another person in sight."

"You sure the Imposters are coming?" Liam asked.

"Hey, I just created the online bread crumb trail," Seth said. "I can't promise they're going to follow it. I mean, I wouldn't if I was this close to launching the auction."

Thanks for that.

"Well, hopefully, the fact that both Holly and I can identify the Ghoul is enough of an incentive," Noah said. "Don't drop your guard."

Showtime. Liam pushed a button on a stereo behind the podium and organ music started playing. The door swung open. Mack and Jess stepped through, both dressed in sleek blue suits. But Noah's eyes locked on the woman standing between them. Dazzling white fabric cascaded down over Holly's form. Her hair was twisted and styled like an old movie star. Drew had done an incredible job. But she could've been wearing blue jeans and a baggy sweater for all he cared. She was beautiful. She was fierce. Her head was held high. But not like a bride on her wedding day. More like a royal figure heading to her execution.

And as she walked up the aisle toward him, he found his heart beating so hard in his chest he couldn't breathe. She reached his side without quite looking at him, and everything inside him wanted her to just turn and meet his eye.

Liam started talking, going through the official words of a wedding service he'd downloaded off the internet. Words about love, words about dedication, loyalty, fidelity and two people standing by each other through thick and thin. Noah's head was spinning. This wasn't working. There was no fire alarm going off or Imposters showing up dressed as firefighters. There were no surprise cops bursting through the door, trying to arrest one of them for an imaginary crime or to report a gas leak.

There was just him, standing beside the very first woman his heart had ever started to fall in love with, pretending they had a relationship they didn't.

He willed Holly to meet his eyes, take his hand and let him know he wasn't alone in this.

"Do you, John Smith, take Hildegard Asher to be your lawful wedded wife?" Liam asked.

"No," Noah said, the single word falling from his lips with a force that shocked him. "Stop the wedding. Or at least give me a minute."

A gasp slipped from Holly's lips, and for the first time since he'd refused to answer her question back at the house she turned and looked him straight in the eye. Irritation flashed in hers. "What are you doing?"

"Can I talk to you privately for a second?"

"Right now?"

"Yes, right now," he said. He glanced at the others. "Please, give us a moment. Just act normal in case we're being watched. The groom's got cold feet."

Questions floated in Holly's eyes. He wished he

knew how to answer them and hoped he wasn't making the biggest mistake of his life. All he knew was he couldn't stand there and do this and pretend to get married—not to Holly—and he didn't know why.

"What's going on?" Seth's panicked voice came through the headset.

"Sorry, guys," Noah said. "I just need to talk to my bride for a moment." He stretched his hand toward Holly. "Let's talk, alone, for just a moment, please."

She nodded. "Okay."

Holly slid her hand into his. They walked out of the main room into a small side room that had once served as the teacher's office.

He closed the door behind them.

"What's going on?" Holly asked. "I know it looks like the sting operation didn't work. But we've only just started. They could still show up before we leave, or be planning something after the ceremony."

"I know," he said, "and we can go back in there and continue fake getting married in a second, and the Imposters might not even realize we took a time-out. But..."

He swallowed hard. Why was this so hard to say?

"But what?" Holly asked, and the simple question seemed to reach inside him and yank at strings he didn't even know he had.

"But this is a wedding," he said. "Which means I'm probably going to kiss you again in a moment. And I need you to know that when I kissed you before it was because I like you. I really, really like you, Holly. I more than like you. Marrying you for pretend, when the idea of marrying a woman like you for real is way beyond even my wildest dreams for my life, just feels really wrong, in a way I can't put into words."

She gasped. Holly stepped forward. Her hand touched his cheek and for a moment Noah actually thought he was about to blurt out that he suspected he was falling in love with her.

"Police!" Liam's voice barked loudly from the other room. "Get down!"

"Down!" Mack snapped at the same time, the two cops' voices bleeding into one. "On the ground! Now!"

"Stay here!" Noah said. He pulled back and placed his hand on Holly's shoulder. "Please! Don't come out until it's over."

He turned away and reached for the door, just as Jess ran in.

"A very belligerent man dressed as a trucker burst through the door," Jess said.

Not what they'd expected, but not surprising.

"Jess, stay here, lock the door and guard Holly," Noah said. Then he turned to her. "Stay with Jess. Lie low and wait for the all clear. Worst case scenario, break out through the window. This room has no door to the outside, but I don't want you to take any unnecessary risks."

Holly's eyes met his, burning with fire and determination. "We should stick together."

"You can't fight in a wedding dress," he said. And he couldn't stand the thought of losing her. "Just stay here. I'll be back in a second."

He turned away and burst through the door, hearing Jess lock it behind him. Then he raised his weapon and turned toward the chaos.

Liam was trying to restrain a large and belliger-ent man, as he bellowed and struggled on the school-house floor. Mack was standing over them, gun at the ready. The front door lay open behind them, sending cold, snowy air blowing through. An unsettled feeling brushed Noah's spine. Even at a distance he could tell it wasn't the Ghoul, let alone the Wraith.

"Noah! What's going on? Tell your guys to let me up."

Noah froze. It was Caleb.

"Guys! Let him up!" Noah ran forward. "It's all over. This is my foster brother."

Liam hesitated for a fraction of a second, just long enough to check Noah's face. Then he let go and stepped back. Mack took a step back, too, but kept his weapon at the ready.

Caleb stumbled to his feet and something in Noah's heart lurched. He'd gained a lot of weight and looked like he hadn't shaved in days. "What kind of greeting is this?"

"I'm sorry." Noah holstered his gun and raised his hands, palms up. He glanced back at the room where Holly was with Jess, thankful, maybe selfishly, that she wasn't witnessing this. "Caleb, I'm sorry. This is not how I wanted our first conversation since the fight to go down. Trust me, this is just a big misunderstand-ing. There's something big going on, and you just got caught up in it."

"Yeah, there's something going on!" Caleb splut-tered. "I hear from Lizzy that you and your fiancée are spending Christmas with Anne and my kids? I hear from Anne we have the opportunity to sell the gym and you won't take it? I hear from the utilities company you got the power and water switched back on at the gym? Then I find out you're getting married and didn't tell me?"

"Because it's not a real wedding, and she's not my real fiancée!" Noah said. "I'm undercover."

And now the operation was beyond destroyed. He'd never imagined Caleb would believe he was really getting married let alone come to town and somehow figure out where the wedding was being held.

Caleb snorted.

"You really going to stand there and lie to my face?" he demanded. "You think Anne didn't tell me you're not on active duty?"

Oh, Lord, help me. I don't even know what to say!

For so long he'd been praying about Caleb, while avoiding the problem and not confronting it. And now it was right here in his face.

"Uh, guys?" Seth's voice crackled in his ear. "There's something weird going on with the online auction timer. It has started speeding up."

"What do you mean, speeding up?" Mack asked.

"Exactly what I said," Seth replied. "It just started going faster."

"Caleb, I'm sorry," Noah said. "Just give me some time and I'll fix this."

"I'm tired of you fixing things!" Caleb shouted. "Don't you get that by now? I don't want you fixing anything! Not my family, not my business, not me! All my life people have been treating me like I'm too useless to do anything. Anne is the only person who's ever believed in me!"

Noah let out a breath. He'd have to let Liam and Mack talk to Seth. He turned to Caleb. It was the worst possible time and the worst possible place, but it looked like they were doing this now.

"I've always believed in you," Noah said.

"No!" Caleb said. "You always tried to be the golden boy. You always tried to save me. You used your poor, pathetic foster brother who needed saving as an excuse for not doing anything with your own existence. You used the fact that I needed you to make me feel bad about myself. You reveled in the fact that my life was a mess, instead of moving on and having a wife, or kids of your own. Because I guess it's easier to save someone else than live your own life! You wouldn't let me run the gym without you looking over my shoulder, telling me what I was doing wrong. You know how I got good at lifting weights back at the gym? Because I actually tried to lift them myself instead of always having you rush in and lift them for me!"

"Well, then I'm really sorry!" Noah said. And as he said the words, he realized he was. "I never meant to make you feel like that. I never meant it to be that way at all. I promise, we'll sit down and talk this all out later. Just not now."

"Guys!" Seth yelped in his ear. "Something's wrong!"

"Don't you try to pull that on me!" Caleb's voice rose. "I know what you're doing! You and your new wife are bringing in new financial partners. You're cutting me out and reopening the gym."

"No," Noah said. "No, that's not what's happening at all! Where did you even get that idea?"

"Guys!" Seth shouted.

Noah turned back toward Liam and Mack. "We have to shut this down. Now!"

"Don't you dare turn your back on me!" Caleb's voice rose. "I saw the emails with the new investors. They contacted me! I know you're going to sue me to cut me out of the deal. I know you told them you'd have me arrested if I even stepped foot inside the place where you were getting married!"

The blood froze in Noah's chest.

"What emails? What investors?" But even as the words crossed his lips, he knew.

Caleb was a distraction. The Imposters knew who Noah really was. The Imposters had emailed his foster brother, gotten him upset and set him up to interrupt the wedding.

"Holly!" Noah spun on his heels and ran for the office. The door handle wouldn't budge. His fists rapped the door. "Holly? Jess? Unlock the door! Open up!"

No answer came from behind it. He tapped his earpiece.

"Seth? It's Noah! What's going on? What did you say about the auction being sped up?" Static crackled through the device. "Liam, find Seth. Mack, take Caleb somewhere safe and debrief him. Tell him whatever you think he needs to know. My cover's been blown and we've been set up!"

He spun back to the door. It was still closed. There was no sound, no motion, nothing but the faintest whiff of something thick and sweet. "Stand back! I'm coming in!"

He kicked the door so hard it flew back on its hinges. The smell of gas filled his nostrils. He wrapped his suit jacket around his mouth and nose. Jess was lying on the floor unconscious. The wide antique floor vent lay open behind her.

Holly was gone.

THIRTEEN

The first sensation that hit Holly as she slowly floated back to consciousness was the realization that the sickly sweet gas that had overwhelmed her senses and dragged her under had now been replaced by stale cold air. Fresh pain was pounding through her head and radiating through her body. She was kneeling, still in the wedding attire, with her head slumped forward and her hands and feet tied behind her, hobbled with her sash, to some kind of rope fencing that gave a little as she moved. She raised her head and looked up.

She was kneeling in the boxing ring in the middle of Bros Gym. Faint winter light filtered through the window. The fluorescent block numbers of the clock on the wall read quarter to eleven. Barely an hour until the auction now.

She opened her mouth to shout, but her voice choked in her throat, probably a side effect of whatever she'd been drugged with. Fear and prayers battled in her heart, as she breathed deeply and waited for her voice to return. She prayed that the auction would be stopped and not a single vulnerable witness would be hurt. She prayed that the Imposters and Snitch5751 would be caught and that General Bertie's crimes would be exposed to the light. She asked God to take care of her parents, her friends, and Anne, Lizzy and Drew. Finally, she prayed for Noah and that God would give him an amazing, incredible life and future with a woman who respected and loved him as much as she did. Then she took a deep breath and pushed her voice past the breaking point and shouted into the gloom.

"Hello!" Her voice echoed in the empty space. "Hello! Is anybody out there?"

"Holly?" The voice was distant, terrified and most definitely Seth's. "Is that you?"

"Seth!" She scanned the room, desperately looking for any sign of the hacker. "Where are you? Are you okay?"

"As all right as a guy can be when there's a bomb strapped to him." His voice quaked. "The Wraith says he'll press the detonator button and blow this whole building if anyone tries to stop him. They launched the auction early. The first name is already on the auction block. Bidding has started."

Dread washed over her aching form. "How do you know?"

Just then a light snapped on above her and she looked up as an eerie sight filled her vision. Seth was tied in a chair, wearing what looked like a bomb vest and sitting at a desk in the open-platform exercise room above. A small screen sat on the table in front of him. Beyond it stood a camera on a tripod, and a production light. A thin figure in a brown delivery uniform sat at another table typing into a computer. It was the Wraith. For a second, she stared at the scene, wondering why they were letting Seth shout at her and see the auction on a screen. Why hadn't he been gagged? Why would they let a hacker watch their crimes? Then Seth's pale and pained face looked down at her almost apologetically and she realized the answer with sickening clarity.

The Imposters had chosen him to be their on-camera victim.

"They're putting you on camera," she called.

"Who better to be the face of an illegal auction than Canada's favorite hacker?" Seth said, weakly.

An electronic bell dinged so loudly the sound seemed to echo through the building. Seth yelped like he'd been electrocuted.

"Seth! Are you okay?"

"The first name's been sold, Holly!" Pain strained Seth's voice to the breaking point. "The first witness's file and secret identity has been sold! Now the second name is up on the auction block."

Dear God, no, please no. Help us stop this.

A figure stepped from the shadows and climbed into the ring, blocking her view of Seth. It was the Ghoul. He'd been there the whole time, she suspected, watching and listening, like a director watching a play from the wings. He was wearing the same nondescript delivery uniform as the Wraith, with his hat pulled low over his eyes.

"We'll figure out who you are," she shouted. "And we'll stop you. I promise."

The Ghoul didn't even flinch. Instead it was like he was looking through her with the same cold, flat expression she'd learned to spot in the face of terrorists who were willing to die as long as they took everyone they could with them.

Was there no humanity left in the Imposters? Had they pretended to be so many other people, and destroyed so many lives, they'd forgotten who they were and how to have compassion? And now, if Seth was right about the bomb, they'd rather blow up the building with themselves inside then get caught. For all his mistakes and faults, when she'd argued with General Bertie she'd seen the angry, conflicted, self-righteous man he was inside. With the Ghoul, all the saw was inhumanity.

She straightened her spine, feeling the muscles in her shoulders and back strain, as the Ghoul walked toward her. His hands rose. In one he held a gun and in the other a cell phone.

The Ghoul stretched the phone out toward her so that she could see the name *Det. Noah Wilder* on the screen. Something flickered in her brain, like the fragment of a memory she had yet to fit within a bigger puzzle.

Lord, help me see what I need to see and remember what I need to remember.

Another chime sounded through the gym. A second witness identity had been sold.

"We're going to call your boyfriend," the Ghoul said. His voice was cold and heartless, and one that would haunt her nightmares. "You're going to tell him exactly what I tell you to, okay?"

So they could send him on a wild-goose chase until the auction was over? So they could trap and kill him somehow?

Her chin rose. "I won't do it."

He could hurt her. He could kill her. But no matter what, she'd die a soldier's death and not lie to the man she cared about.

"You will do what I say." The Ghoul stepped closer. The phone floated before her face, like a rectangle of light burning her eyes. "Or you will die painfully and alone."

"I'd rather die alone than die a traitor."

The Ghoul hit a button. The phone rang. A loud and raucous rock-and-roll riff reverberated down the hallway, filling the gym with noise.

Her heart swelled. She wasn't alone. Noah was there. He'd found her.

The Ghoul spun toward the sound and fired down the hall. Holly lunged, feeling her arms ache and her shoulders strain as blinding pain shot through her limbs. The wedding sash tore in two and she flew forward, throwing herself at her captor and catching him in the knees. The Ghoul fell out of the ring. His gun clattered somewhere in the darkness. She crawled forward. Her feet were still tied to the ropes behind her, and her wrists were still tangled in the sash. She couldn't see the Ghoul anywhere.

"Holly!" Noah was pelting down the hall toward her.

"Stop!" she shouted. "The Wraith is upstairs with Seth. He has Seth rigged to a bomb and says he'll blow up the building if anyone tries to stop him. Go save Seth and stop the auction. Two lives have already been sold! I'll be okay!"

For one agonizing second, she watched Noah hesitate and a million unspoken thoughts and feelings fill his face. She loved this man. She knew it now without a doubt. Now she just prayed he trusted her.

A third sale pinged. Another life had been stolen.

"Go now!" She yanked the fabric from her wrists, then turned around, shoving the skirt of the wedding dress out of her way and trying to free her ankles. "Each time that sound goes it means another life's been sold. Every second you wait, another person could die. Go! Stop the auction, save Seth and defuse the bomb. Then come get me!"

Steel and tears burned in his eyes. "Promise me you're going to stay alive until I get back!"

"I do!"

Noah turned and ran for the stairs. She kicked her feet, feeling the fabric tear.

The Ghoul lunged over the side of the boxing ring and leaped at her.

Noah bounded up the stairs to the second floor, feeling his heart crack and splinter a little more with each step. Behind him he could hear Holly fighting for her life. *Save her, Lord! Keep her alive. Please, don't let her get hurt. I don't want to imagine my life without her in it.*

He rounded a corner and reached the athletic studio. There, he saw Seth, bound to a chair, dressed in an explosives vest and sitting in front of a computer screen. The Wraith was at another desk typing on a laptop. There was black detonator switch in his hand. Seth flashed Noah a weak and terrified smile. Noah turned to the Wraith and raised his weapon. "I don't want to hurt you. Please just stop the auction and let Seth go."

Wraith snorted and hit a key on the laptop. A ding sounded. "Every step you take, every time you even move, I'll release another person's file, free to the first person to bid on it," he said.

Noah rolled his shoulders back. "This doesn't have to end badly. You can just get up and walk away."

The Wraith hit another key. Another ding sounded. "That's five lives, Detective. Five people whose identities have been sold. Turn around and walk away yourself, or I'll release them all."

"Seth?" Noah turned to his friend. "I believe in you."

Then he turned to the Wraith.

"Stop. The. Auction! Now!" Noah raised his weapon and aimed it at his chest. "I don't want to shoot you. I really don't. But I will if I have to."

The Wraith laughed and slapped the laptop. Loud dinging filled the room, like half a dozen elevators all stopping at once. Every ping was another life being destroyed.

Lord, have mercy.

"I'm the only one who can stop this auction now." The Wraith's hand moved over the detonator switch. "You so much as move and I'll blow this whole place, taking us all with it and there'll be nothing you can do to stop it."

Noah fired. His bullet struck the Wraith in the chest. The Imposter crumpled to the floor, dead. The detonator fell from his hand. Noah ran for Seth, grabbed his knife, cut the hacker free from the chair and helped him out of the explosives vest. "You got this, right?"

"Absolutely." Seth leaped up, sending the chair crashing behind him. He ran for the laptop.

"Seth—"

"I know!" His hands flew over the keys. "Hack the

encryption, stop the auction, delete the data, make sure the bomb doesn't have some kind of a fail-safe backup and if it does defuse it too, and also call in everyone possible in law enforcement. I'm on it. Run! Go save Holly!"

Noah turned and dashed from the room, prayers for help and of thanksgiving pouring through him at every step. He reached the stairs and flew down them, his heart aching when he reached the hallway and saw the scene unfolding before him. Holly had jumped or been thrown from the ring and was now on the gym floor on her back, struggling and kicking at the Ghoul as he tried to choke the life from her lungs.

Dimly, Noah registered the fact that the pinging had stopped. The auction was over.

The Ghoul yanked Holly up by her neck like a rag doll and held her in front of him.

"Let her go!" Noah shouted. "It's over! The auction has ended! Your partner is dead! Step away from her! Hands on your head! Now!"

The Ghoul tossed Holly to the ground. She landed on her stomach, bounced and lay there. Then the thug turned and charged at him.

Noah raised his gun and pulled the trigger. His weapon jammed. But a second bullet cracked the air a fraction of a second later. The Ghoul fell, and Noah looked past him to where Holly stood in the tattered wedding dress, over the criminal's body with the Ghoul's smoking gun in her hands.

It *was* over.

Holly ran for Noah and landed in his arms. He clutched her to his chest, letting the warmth of her fill his core. For a moment, he was lost in the feeling of having her there, of holding her to him and of her clutching him to her, breathing in the relief of being together. Then he heard the sounds of sirens roaring outside and the shouts of law enforcement officials pelting down the hall, with Liam, Mack and Jess leading the way.

"Come on," Noah said. He slid away from Holly just enough to put his arm around her shoulders. "Let's brief the team, leave them in charge and grab a quick moment alone, away from the chaos. There's something I need to say."

She nodded. "Deal."

They ran toward the team, filled them in, and then helped direct the cops to the Wraith and the Ghoul. Noah saw Seth stumble down the stairs and watched as his friends took control of the scene. Then Noah and Holly pressed through a side door and out into the snow. They stood there for a moment in the relative calm and peace, feeling the snow brush their bodies.

"I'm never wearing a skirt again," she said, after a long moment. "Ever. I think I've also developed an allergy to flashing lights and emergency sirens. I can't wait to get rid of all this hair."

He chuckled. "I don't blame you."

"Before you ask, my head feels terrible," she said. She turned toward him. "Thank you for trusting me, turning around and running to stop the auction. Every second we delayed could've cost someone their life."

"I know, and Seth is the one who stopped the auction. I just saved Seth." His hands slid around her shoulders and he pulled her to his chest. "Thank you for staying alive until I reached you."

"Anytime." A smile crossed her lips and warmed something in his heart.

He lowered his face toward her, letting his lips brush hers in a kiss.

"There you are!" Seth called. "Auction's done and the bomb was easy enough to defuse."

Noah pulled back but didn't let go of Holly.

"How many of the stolen identities were sold before the auction was stopped?" she asked.

Seth's face paled. "Sixteen."

Holly's eyes closed. "Lord, have mercy."

"We'll save them," Noah said. "I'm going to take that promotion. I'm going to recommend Seth for a position in Cyber and track down each criminal buyer. Liam, Mack and Jess will go back out in the field. We'll find and help every single one of them before the criminals from their past can reach them. We'll help them find new lives."

God had blessed him with an amazing team. Together, they'd make sure every person on that list was safe.

"Can you give us a moment?" Noah asked.

"I would," Seth said. "But there's something really major going down that Holly's going to want to see. Like, right now."

He held up his phone, open to a media site. Holly let go of Noah and took it with both hands. Noah looked over her shoulder. It was a news conference. General Bertie Frey was standing at a podium in front of a group of reporters, surrounded by other members of her military unit and his closest aids. His arm was in a sling from the Ghoul's bullet.

"I had an alert set up to let me know if Bertie did

anything," Seth explained. "Apparently, he called a press conference today. We missed the first fifteen minutes, but I can start it from the beginning when it's done."

Her eyebrows rose. "On Christmas Eve? Why?"

"He's confessing," Seth said.

"To what?" Holly asked.

"Everything," Seth said. "Judging by the news scroll. He's admitted to bartering and selling weapons, falsifying records and lying to investigators. I don't know what went on between you and him yesterday, but apparently whatever you said or did, or the fact that you saved his life, gave him a pretty big change of heart."

Seth pushed a button and the general's voice filled the air.

"...I'm prepared to make a full and complete accounting of my actions to the parliamentary inquiry and law enforcement," Bertie was saying. "I want to apologize to God, my family, my colleagues and all those I lied to and who were impacted by my actions. I also want to apologize deeply and sincerely to Corporal Hildegard Asher for the horrible position I put her in and the reprehensible way people treated her because of my actions. She is a hero, a soldier and a patriot, who deserved to be lauded for her courage and not threatened by cowards who believed they were acting on my behalf. Finally, to the family of my dear friend Detective Elias Crane, I am so sorry for his loss..."

"Elias was behind this," Holly said suddenly. She glanced from Noah to Seth and back again. "Bertie just called him a close personal friend, which means taking on my protection was a conflict of interest. He all but told me he thought Bertie's crimes were no big deal. You told me he'd requested to transport me. He had access to everything Snitch5751 gave the Imposters. Those facts alone would've put him top of the suspect list if the Imposters hadn't killed him. It would explain why Snitch5751 hasn't sent anything else since the accident." She glanced at Seth. "Is this a live feed?"

"Yeah." He nodded.

"We text him, right now," she said, "tell them it's me, that I'm watching and ask him if Elias Crane was at his country house the same day and time Snitch5751 messaged the Imposters."

What was she thinking? Was she really about to do this while Bertie was live on television? And yet Noah trusted her, like he did his own heartbeat.

"Here." Noah reached into his pocket. "Use my phone."

"Thank you," she said. She took the phone from his hand and started typing. "And yes, I know he probably has the discipline not to glance at his phone during a news briefing. But that's why we also text everyone other member of my unit who's standing around him in that room right now, too. I've served with every single person on that screen right now, and I can tell you several of them will at least glance at their phones. Eventually one of them will nudge him."

"All right," Noah said. It was worth a try.

She hit Send.

They all watched in real time as a round of pings sounded in the crowd. The general flinched. Sure enough he didn't check his phone, but several around him surreptitiously glanced at theirs. Finally the sergeant to his left leaned over and whispered something in Bertie's ear. He glanced down at the man's phone.

Holly typed another line, turning the phone so Noah could read it on the screen. Please, General. I told you what those men did to me. Is it possible Elias sent them?

Bertie's face paled. Reporters were shouting questions now. The general raised his hand.

"One more thing I'd like to add," he said. "Corporal Asher suffered a reprehensible attack at the hands of three men, which led her into witness protection. It has since been drawn to my attention that it's possible the person who arranged that evil act was a personal friend who did so from a device that was connected to my Wi-Fi at the time. While I didn't think anything of it then, I did have an ill-advised and regrettable conversation with that friend, in which he said he wished there was something he could do to encourage Corporal Asher to keep her mouth shut." His eyes locked on the camera, but it was like he was gazing through the screen directly at her. "I will do everything in my power to enable investigators looking into that possibility. No more questions. Thank you."

The news conference ended. Seth stopped the video.

"That's as close as I think we're going to get to a confession for now," Seth said. "But I'll start digging into the Elias Crane is Snitch5751 theory immediately. It shouldn't take much to prove."

Holly's knees buckled, her head dropped into her hands and her shoulders shook.

"Hey." Noah reached for her, gently rubbing his palm between her shoulder blades. "It's going to be okay."

She looked up at him. Fierce tears shone in her eyes.

"What if that's it?" she asked. "What if it's finally over?"

He ran his hands down her arms until his fingers touched hers. But she didn't grasp them. Instead, she stood up and shook her head, tossing the ragged mess of long, fake hair around her shoulders. "General Bertie has confessed and called off the attack dogs. The Imposters have been stopped. The auction is over. I'm free. I can go back on active duty. I can be deployed. I can get back to my life."

Noah's heart sank in his chest. Yes, she could, she would, and he was happy for her for that. Yet the thought of Holly leaving made something ache so painfully in his chest it was as if she'd reached inside him and taken his heart with her.

She ran both hands through her hair and turned toward the door. "I should go. I have to go talk to investigators and get back to base. I've been away far too long."

"Wait," Noah said. Holly stopped and turned back. He turned to glance at Seth, and only then realized the hacker had already discreetly slipped back into the building. "Don't go. Not yet. Let me celebrate Christmas and your birthday with you tomorrow. Let's spend a few days together, before you go back. You're still recovering from a concussion."

"Which I can do better in my own home," she said, "on base, under the care of a military doctor. I'm caught up in two major investigations, Noah. I can't put off doing my duty for a few days just because I'm tired."

"Then do it because I'm not ready to say goodbye to you yet." Noah reached for her hands and this time she didn't pull away. "Stay because I think you're the most extraordinary person I've ever met. I think you're dazzling, tenacious, driven and brave. My heart did backflips when I saw you walk down the aisle this morning, because I realized I never want to see myself standing at an altar beside anyone else as long as I live." His fingers linked through hers. He pulled her closer until their lips were only a breath or two apart. "It scares me to say this, because I've never said it to anyone before, but I think I'm falling in love with you, Holly. I'm hoping with every beat of my foolish heart you feel the same way about me, too. Do you?"

Okay, he'd done it. He'd been foolish and he'd been brave. Now all he could do was hope and pray she felt the same way.

But she didn't answer. For a long time she just stood there, toe to toe with him, heart to heart, her hands holding his and her eyes searching his as if looking for something so lost she'd almost given up hope of finding it.

Then she stepped away.

"No," she said softly. "I'm sorry, Noah. I'm not ready to say that I do. I can't stand here in somebody else's wedding dress, with fake eyes and fake hair, pretending to be someone I'm not, and tell a man I only met six days ago that I love him."

She let go of his hands and pressed her fingers against her eyes as if to block the tears. His mouth opened, but his chest was so tight he couldn't speak a word.

"I don't believe in love at first sight," she said. "You know that about me. I never have and maybe I never will. To me love has to be a solid thing that grows slowly, based on far more than some fluttering in my chest—even if right now it feels my heart is beating so hard it hurts to breathe. You've barely met me, and you don't really know me."

"Maybe not," he said. "But this feels real. I feel something for you, Holly. Something I've never felt before. Do you really feel nothing for me?"

"Noah, I feel everything for you." She swallowed hard. "But I can't risk my entire life on my feelings like this and neither should you. And because of that, I have to go now, before I say, do or promise something that will lead us down a path we'll both one day end up regretting."

She leaned forward, kissed him goodbye, and for one long moment they clung to each other. Then slowly, Holly pulled away. "Goodbye, Noah, I'm going to miss you so much more than you'll ever know."

Then the first woman who'd ever opened up Noah's heart turned and walked away.

FOURTEEN

Red and green lights shone softly on the Reed family tree, casting a gentle glow over Drew and Lizzy as they lay on their stomachs on the living room floor, surrounded by the remnants of wrapping paper, and carefully assembled the train set Caleb had gotten Lizzy for Christmas. Noah sat in the overstuffed armchair by the fire and looked out at the snow gently buffeting the world outside.

Carols flowed from the refurbished record player on the mantel and mostly succeeded in blocking out Anne's and Caleb's voices coming from the kitchen, where they were putting the finishing touches on Christmas dinner. Seemed like the two of them had been talking nonstop ever since Anne and the kids had returned to the house the afternoon before. Sometimes they'd sat quietly, talking in hushed voices and holding each other's hands. Other times they'd argued so loudly that Noah, Drew and Lizzy had thrown their boots and coats on and gone sledding until the conversation had died down. But at least Caleb had stayed, and he and Anne were talking. And Noah thanked God for that.

Whatever the story of Caleb and Anne's love would end up being, it seemed this Christmas wasn't the day they'd have all the answers. But Noah had agreed to let Caleb and the gym go, and trust that whatever he did with his share of the money, and whatever roads his foster brother went down, those were his choices to make. The three of them had come to a compromise. They'd sell the gym to the buyer Anne had found. Caleb's share of the money would be split into four equal parts, providing Anne with a quarter for herself and a quarter in trust for each of Drew's and Lizzy's future education. Noah prayed that one day the rift between him and Caleb would be healed, and that God would continue to work in all their lives. But Holly had been right. It was time to stop trying to save Caleb.

Noah had no idea how long it would take his own heart to heal from saying goodbye to Holly. They'd spoken again briefly and politely, surrounded by law enforcement officers, before she'd finally gotten into a waiting car and driven out of his life.

Since then, thanks to General Bertie's cooperation, Seth had confirmed that Elias Crane had been Snitch5751, by uncovered emails and even a money trail, proving Elias had hired the attackers who terrorized Holly into accepting witness protection, and then pulled strings to make sure he was assigned to her case. Seth had also uncovered proof that Elias had been working with the Imposters in exchange for a large cash payout to soften his imminent retirement and the promise that Holly would disappear. But there was no indication Elias knew what they were going to use the data they collected for, or that they would kill him to cover their tracks. Both Imposters had died from their wounds and their true identities had been revealed as a pair of fraternal twins from Squamish, British Columbia. And although he now knew who they were, Noah and his colleagues had agreed not to speak or even think their names and were pushing media outlets not to provide them with the notoriety they might've craved. People like that didn't deserve infamy for their crimes. They deserved to be forgotten. Especially as RCMP officers were still working around the clock at Christmas to protect, reassure and rehouse all those whose lives and identities had been stolen.

Maybe Caleb had been partly right that Noah had used helping him as an excuse for not stepping up to live his own life. And now, for the first time he could remember, his life lay ahead of him like an open road, with endless possibilities. And while he was excited to take them and see where they might lead, he couldn't get past the feeling that something was missing.

That the most important piece of the puzzle was absent.

The sound of tires crunched on the snow outside. He glanced out. The vehicle was military. The young man behind the wheel was uniformed and sat straight. But it was the woman in the passenger seat who had him leaping from his seat, shoving his feet into boots, flinging the door wide and running outside without waiting to do up his coat.

Holly wore military fatigues. Her hair had been cut short in a pixie cut that highlighted her cheekbones and the lines of her face. Her skin was free of makeup and the light that shone in her eyes was more beautiful than any sight he'd seen in his life.

"Holly!" Noah ran to her, arms outstretched to welcome her as she rushed into them, and for a long moment he just held her there, lost in the feeling of her in his arms. "I'm so sorry for what I said yesterday, if I offended you or spoke out of turn..."

"No, it's okay." She pulled back and looked in his face but kept her arms around his body. "We're different people. We say and feel things in different ways. And the fact that you want to love me is the most incredible thing that's ever happened to me."

What was she saying?

She swallowed hard. "I've decided not to deploy back overseas and applied for a transfer for a position training new recruits outside Ottawa. I still feel served to call my country, but everything I've gone through in the past few days—getting to know Seth, Anne and Drew, thinking about the people whose lives the Imposters threatened, and what you've told me about growing up in a fostering home—has given me this desire to make a difference here, back home in Canada. There's a lot of hurt and a lot of need here. The military will always be my family, one of them anyway, and I think I want to make a difference by helping other kids who need a family find belonging and purpose there, and to encourage the military to be more welcoming and inclusive to people who want to serve their country. Plus, like it or not, thanks to Bertie's press conference I'm a bit of a celebrity now, at least for a few weeks until the news move on to something else. And I'm going to use that platform to stand up for what I believe in."

Something swelled in his heart. Did she have any idea how incredible she was? Not just in terms of outside, surface beauty, but in how passionately she cared and how deep her desire and drive was to serve others?

"That sounds amazing," he said. "I think you'll be incredible at that, and anyone would be a fool not to listen to you."

Happy tears gleamed in her eyes.

"Thank you," she said. "Also, that means I'm relocating to Ottawa, which means we have time to grow together. I told you yesterday that I didn't believe a week-long relationship was enough to promise forever on. But I was wrong if I implied I hadn't seen enough to know how much I really want to."

Her hands slid up into his hair. His breath caught in his chest.

"What are you saying, Holly?"

"I've seen how you treat people and how you treat me," she said. "I've seen how you admit when you're wrong, stand up for what you believe in, deal with people who disagree with you and ask when you need help. I've seen how brave, loving, courageous, compassionate and strong you are. I know you well enough to know I want to get to know you better, slowly, deeply and forever. I'm in love for the first time in my life, and it's with you, Noah. And while I want to take it slow, I'm really hoping that we're going to be side by side, loving each other and having each other's backs for the rest of our lives."

Joy filled his heart, spilling a smile across his face. "I think we will."

"Me, too."

"Happy Birthday, Holly. I love you so much."

"Merry Christmas, Noah. I love you, too."

And he wrapped his arms around her and kissed the woman he knew without a doubt that he was going to love forever.

* * * * *

If you enjoyed this story, look for these other titles by Maggie K. Black from Love Inspired Suspense:

The Littlest Target
Undercover Holiday Fiancé
Rescuing His Secret Child

Dear Reader,

Welcome to the first book of my new Stolen Identities series. I hope you enjoy it! The best part of writing the True North Heroes and True North Protectors series was getting to know the characters better as I watched their lives crisscross each other's stories. Now I'm excited to do it again in this new witness protection series, while bringing back both Liam Bearsmith and Seth Miles for more adventures.

I wrote this book while recovering from a concussion. During the slow recovery, I realized my usual way of sitting down and writing a book wasn't working, and so I had to come up with new strategies. I owe a huge debt of thanks to my editor, Emily Rodmell, and agent, Melissa Jeglinski, for their patience and help in getting my writing back on track.

I hope that whatever you're going through, you are surrounded by people who support and love you. And that when needed, God will help you find those people and bring them into your life.

Thank you again, as always, for sharing this journey with me.

Maggie

Get 4 FREE REWARDS!

We'll send you 2 FREE Books plus 2 FREE Mystery Gifts.

Love Inspired® Suspense books feature Christian characters facing challenges to their faith... and lives.

FREE Value Over $20

"Come in," Katie Jameson called, bracing herself for the meeting with Dr. Ritter.

The door swung open and a man in a white lab coat stepped in, holding her chart close to his face.

Only, he was not the doctor she was expecting.

Dr. Ritter was in his early sixties with salt-and-pepper hair and enough extra weight to fill out his lab coat. The doctor who was moving toward her had dark hair and a muscular build. His scuffed shoes and baggy lab coat made her wonder if he were a resident at the hospital where she would be giving birth.

"Good morning," she said. She had been meeting with Dr. Ritter since the beginning of the pregnancy. He understood her feelings about the birth. Talking about the fact that Jordan wouldn't be around for his daughter's birth, her childhood, her life always brought her close to the tears she despised.

"Morning," he mumbled.

"Is Dr. Ritter running late?" she asked, uneasiness joining the unsettled feeling in the pit of her stomach.

"He won't be able to make it," the man said, lowering the charts and grinning.

She went cold with terror.

She knew the hazel eyes, the lopsided grin, the high forehead. "Martin," she stammered.

"Sorry it took me so long to get to you, sweetheart. I had to watch from a distance until I was certain we could be alone."

"Watch?"

"They wanted to keep me in the hospital, but our love is too strong to be denied. I escaped for you. For us." He lifted a hand, and if she had not jerked back, his fingers would have brushed her cheek.

He scowled. "Have they brainwashed you? Have they turned you against me?"

"You did that yourself when you murdered my husband," she responded.

Don't miss
Sworn to Protect *by Shirlee McCoy,*
available November 2019 wherever
Love Inspired® Suspense books and ebooks are sold.

www.LoveInspired.com

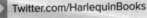